About the author

John Goddard, retired after many years as an English teacher, is the author of *Conversations with Clocks* and *Smoke Gets in Your Eyes* and now turns his hand to his favourite genre, mystery detective stories. He lives in the Blue Mountains west of Sydney, and as well as writing, spends time on his church and on children and grandchildren in the Sydney area and in Wales.

The Pool of Siloam

John Goddard

The Pool of Siloam

Vanguard Press

VANGUARD PAPERBACK

© Copyright 2023
John Goddard

The right of John Goddard to be identified as author of
this work has been asserted by him in accordance with the
Copyright, Designs and Patents Act 1988.

All Rights Reserved

No reproduction, copy or transmission of this publication
may be made without written permission.
No paragraph of this publication may be reproduced,
copied or transmitted save with the written permission of the
publisher, or in accordance with the provisions
of the Copyright Act 1956 (as amended).

Any person who commits any unauthorised act in relation to
this publication may be liable to criminal
prosecution and civil claims for damages.

A CIP catalogue record for this title is
available from the British Library.

ISBN 978-1-80016-609-7

*Vanguard Press is an imprint of
Pegasus Elliot Mackenzie Publishers Ltd.*
www.pegasuspublishers.com

First Published in 2023

**Vanguard Press
Sheraton House Castle Park
Cambridge England**

Printed & Bound in Great Britain

I

If only they had known that there was catastrophe to follow, they would not have been in such a hurry to set out.

The bus left the college soon after six on Saturday morning, Fred Jones driving a group of twenty-one staff and students. The morning was still and calm. The sun was not yet up, and so the students decided that a continuation of their interrupted night's rest was in order. They constituted most of the Geology and Geography classes of the senior years and they were on their way to the Blue Mountains west of Sydney, a field trip to study erosion, rock formations, unusual settlement patterns and even, just possibly, Wollemi pines. "One never knew," said Bill Dawson, the senior Geography teacher, "what opportunities would present themselves in a wild and unfamiliar area." He should have known better — they would be many miles away from those ancient, elusive and well-guarded pines — but he was an optimist, and the mere thought, Wollemi, stirred him in strange ways. He hoped it was so for others. Guy Somerville, the geology specialist, smiled benevolently at him and made more sensible plans.

An early start, in the gloom of a college morning, when the rest of the student population were still cosily in bed, having already begun their holidays, had perhaps engendered an odd mix of brief enthusiasm and mild regret. If such a mix existed, it was quickly followed, when the travellers realised how long the day's journey would be, by a determination to return to sleep. For a time, Felicity Madigan maintained vigilance, as she thought was required of the senior staff member of the expedition; Matron South, it may be assumed, was never off duty. Nevertheless, it was not long before nature took its course, and Fred Jones drove, lost in his own genial thoughts and uninterrupted by those of his passengers, for upwards of three hours. Their drive was almost all on what amounted to motorway, until a massive roadhouse and the sudden realisation that a toilet stop was urgently needed brought about a halt. Felicity Madigan jerked into action, and as acting deputy at the college, gave the order, as much in hope as in expectation. "We move off in twenty minutes. Don't hold us up." Twenty-two people headed for food and conveniences.

"I could use a hash brown, or three," beamed Fred as he locked the bus.

"The coffee had better be reasonable — I can't hope for much more than just reasonable, I suppose," murmured Felicity.

"A good cup of tea, that's all I need," offered Matron South, though her tone made it plain that these ugly but useful roadhouses would not supply tea that she considered acceptable. She hardly knew what to make of this, for her, most unusual excursion. There had to be a matron in the party, she knew that, so that regular college care could be maintained; she was grateful that Felicity Madigan, the senior English teacher as well as acting deputy and neither a geographer nor a geologist, had agreed to sacrifice a week of holiday so that Matron would not be the only female in the party. Another woman, and a sensible one at that, would be in charge; this was undoubtedly good and reassuring in Matron's eyes. But even Felicity's presence did not allay her doubts about an acceptable cup of tea.

About a fortnight before this day, it had become apparent that, for various reasons, including the cost, which college people preferred not to mention, there would be two spare spaces on the bus. In a spirit of great generosity, Headmaster Parslow had insisted that those spaces be offered to two visitors from Chaddlehangar school, near Tavistock in the south-west of England. There was Mr Dennis Millane, an English teacher coming to the end of a twelve-month exchange with one of the college's teachers, Doug Anderson. Millane had been very well received at the college. Together with his wife and child, he had entered enthusiastically into all that a year in a foreign country can be supposed to offer. They had travelled widely, had been entertained lavishly, and before term had ended, had held a thank-you entertainment and drinks in their tiny college house.

But Amanda Millane and her four-year-old son were not part of the present excursion. They were spending a quiet week at the college before their winding path home took them via India and Malta. She needed, she said, to work up her strength for the gruelling program her husband had designed. And what would be the use of a child on a geological expedition? — No, Dennis would go and leave her in peace.

The other spare spot on the bus was occupied by Roger Xanthius, a former student of Chaddlehangar school. This loose-limbed and handsome young man, still only nineteen years of age, had arrived in the college in the preceding January for six months' work experience. Headmaster Parslow, who harboured severe doubts about the wisdom of allowing young men to be part of the staff when they were barely more than students themselves, had reluctantly agreed to accept Xanthius as an inevitable part, almost, of the teacher exchange deal. Perhaps it would have been mean to refuse such a polite request and the fellow had helped out in sport, not very well, and in library supervision, more or less satisfactorily, and as a member of the photography club. In this role he was little short of brilliant. He was much more than a keen photographer. His work on the flora and fauna of the college was beautiful and he also had the knack of snapping action shots of swimmers or footballers at just the right moment. He too was to leave Australia soon after the Blue Mountains excursion, in his case on a direct flight to London, and the offer of a place on the bus was in one obvious sense a vote of thanks for the truly excellent photographs he left behind for the college to use as they wished.

At the roadhouse, six staff members, armed with coffee or tea and perhaps some more solid kinds of refreshment, sat at one table. The fifteen students, plus Roger, sat themselves here and there, some eagerly awake, some barely out of that slumberous state which a long drive on an uninteresting country motorway can induce. Roger, who claimed that hot chips in Australia were both crisper and fluffier than any you could get in the UK, was working his way through an enormous pile, having duly photographed them first.

"How can you get away with such heaps of chips?" complained Arty. "Look at you — you're a scarecrow!"

"I get away with it out of sheer determination," came the smiling reply.

Boys at seventeen do not want to be thought tubby, but Arty was and he knew it. Perhaps that was why the young Englishman, not much older than himself, fascinated Arty. Roger looked splendid, certainly, but what was even more important in Arty's eyes, he would have a go at anything, and then could speak carelessly of both his successes and his failures. It was not normal college behaviour, and if Xanthius had seemed sometimes to teeter on the edge of un-college attitudes, he had certainly formed a small coterie of thorough admirers. They would be sorry, they said, for such a fresh breeze to blow no more.

So Roger devoured his chips and Arty Fulsom and Shu Brillia looked on in delighted astonishment. Shu was a gifted student for whom the foundations of this earth were as poems in stone and he was eagerly anticipating some remarkable sights in the Blue Mountains, which he had never seen. A substantial scholarship enabled him to attend the college and the current field trip had stretched his family's financial reserves very tightly. He had convinced his parents that such an expedition would show them all whether some aspect of earth science would be his future career. He had to prove himself worthy, of both parents and school, yet there was Roger.

"I'll be taking photos, Roger, but I hope you'll let me have copies of yours. They'll be better."

"Will they be better for your science — or just prettier?"

"If they are the second, they'll probably be the first as well."

Roger smiled complacently, then, "Bus leaves in three minutes, move along," was heard and a final toilet rush followed. But Felicity Madigan was not displeased: the entire stop had taken barely thirty minutes.

It had been a gruelling term at the college — is there any other kind, in teachers' eyes? — and the staff members in particular were content to sit back in idle thought as the bus cruised north. They did not so readily resort to headphones plugged into mobile phones or into other devices in order to shut out the world as the students did, but they felt just as inward. Perhaps Dennis Millane was somewhat more tourist-minded than the others but there was, in truth, little to excite the observer. So he, like the others, marked off the major stages of the journey and thought mainly of his return to Chaddlehangar, of picking up well-known courses of study and trusting that the Anderson fellow had not done too much damage in the interim. He was supremely confident in his own abilities and knowledge in the field of English teaching, and from what he had seen at the college, doubted that any of the colonials had anything like his depth and wisdom. He found that he could respect Felicity Madigan, the Head of English as well as acting deputy, but the others seemed to him to be merely competent. It must say something, he thought, of the essential weakness of the Australian system that, with such teaching, the college students consistently scored very well in the state-wide examinations. It did not occur to him to reason the other way around. He had enjoyed the year — but he was greatly looking forward to being back home, to a well-known and well-ordered environment. Chaddlehangar was the world he knew.

One particular aspect of the last six months had irked him and made him keen for his Australian adventure to conclude — Roger Xanthius. It had been assumed that he would in some sense be Roger's mentor or minder. But Roger, he knew, was not a person to be mentored, much less minded, by anybody. What was worse, Roger's erratic brilliance and his streak of rebelliousness had reflected back on Dennis himself, as though all Chaddlians were like that. They were not. Nevertheless, he had been expected to keep an eye on camera-happy Roger and see to it that he came to no harm. Their time together — and they had never had much to do with each other at Chaddlehangar — was almost over and Dennis could feel only immense relief. There was no reason he would ever cross the young man's path again. Let him go off to university or on a grand tour, if that was what his messed-up family wanted — they could certainly afford it! — and all this absurd mentoring would be finished. Excellent!

"It will be a late lunch," came the voice of Fred Jones. He must have wanted to stir the sleeping, because he continued in a most animated voice, "And here's a little song to get you in the mood." There was a guitar introduction and then a somewhat whining country and western voice, which is to say a typical country and western voice, told them about a track winding back to an old-fashioned shack, and so forth.

"Nostalgia," muttered Felicity Madigan, "for those of us who are over eighty. But I hardly think…"

"Wasn't that great!" came in Fred. "And we'll shortly be stopping about five miles from Gundagai and you can see for yourselves that statue of the little dog sitting on the tuckerbox. It's a beaut spot."

"No, it isn't!" said Felicity to Matron, with unusual bluntness. "Or not any more. It looks sad and uninteresting and overrun by the food outlets. And anyway," and here she raised her voice to Fred, "the dog is in a different poem. That's not the one Slim Dusty was singing."

"It's still Gundagai," chortled the irrepressible Jones. "It's grand country!"

Felicity looked out at the arid undulations all around. There must, she thought, be a peculiarly Australian kind of optimism that saw grandeur in what they were passing through. Then they came to the stretch over the Murrumbidgee. Perhaps the spread, the sheer space of it all was impressive, but the endless Hume, Melbourne to Sydney, was not her idea of grand at all.

The lunch stop was indescribably boring. Roger livened things up a little by arranging photos of his friends patting or making faces at the dog on its tuckerbox, and he even got an obviously vexed Millane to join Arty and Shu, the boys pretending to prevent their teacher from strangling the dog. It will be over soon, Millane said to himself, then he felt grumpier, more vexed than ever, when he walked to the bus past a gentleman who gave him a withering look and muttered something about "showing more respect and who did these pommies think they were, anyway?"

"Just a bit of fun, Mr Millane," but Dennis was no longer in the mood for Roger's brand of fun. He had vowed to look after the young man and wondered now how he had come to be saddled with such a burden. But he said to himself, he would not shirk the issue. An unwelcome responsibility was still a responsibility and he meant to take it seriously.

More of the Hume, and still more, with one more toilet break, and it was all of five o'clock when they branched onto the Northern Road and finally the Great Western Highway to take them to the Blue Mountains. Dinner, they were told, would be pizza and salad at their motel in Katoomba, the principal town from which their daily excursions and walks would commence. It was part traditional motel and part bunkhouse, so that the fifteen students were to sleep in two large dormitory-style rooms and the staff in adjacent twin-share motel accommodation. As always, sighed Dennis Millane, this brought up the ambiguous status of Roger Xanthius.

No, Felicity had said before the trip even began, he is not a student and is not to be put in a student dormitory. He would have to share with a staff member, to which the men most vigorously objected. Somerville and Dawson intended to share, as the two teachers most concerned with the learning content of the trip; both Millane and Jones flatly refused. As a consequence, those two men shared and Roger was offered a small double all to himself. He found this arrangement perfectly satisfactory. He would be by himself, with enough space to sort through his photos away from anyone's inspection. And he would not be far from the dormitories, where he hoped to find, or to engineer, some fun.

"Keep an eye on him, please, Dennis. He can't go in amongst the boys for the night," was Madigan's injunction.

"I hope you don't expect either Fred or me to be on Roger watch until two am," came back Millane. "Do you not trust him, then?"

Felicity chose not to reply. Then, "Please keep an eye, and an ear, open," she said and joined Somerville and Dawson for a quick briefing before bed. A long day of doing nothing she found very tiring. She hoped the others felt the same — that they would sleep well and that, like her, they wanted to experience something more stimulating on the morrow.

II

If Day One had been essentially sedentary, Day Two was intended to be not overly vigorous either. The teachers had decided on a gentle introduction to the famous area. So the students spent the morning in the obvious ways: a film called The Edge which whisked them through canyons and over precipices so convincingly that Bart Springside dashed out to be sick, and then some time at the Three Sisters, undoubtedly the most recognisable rock formation in the whole area. They clambered down to the first sister, then down more and more to a path hundreds of feet below.

"It will be fun coming back up," groaned Cec Bickerly, but the boy cheered up enormously when he discovered that Mr Somerville, in his careful planning, had arranged that the ascent back up was in fact on a scenic railway, an incredibly steep contraption that hauled them back up to Scenic World, with its skyway above a terrifying drop and the inevitable tourist shop.

"Look at your photos tonight," advised Somerville, "keep it all in your minds and then tomorrow, when we've done Wentworth Falls, we'll introduce you to the field study assignments that flow from all this."

He would have been disappointed if there had not been moans.

"What! You didn't think this was a tourist's holiday, did you?" Then, with triumphant glee, "This is work!"

After Scenic World, Jones drove them to Govett's Leap but by then the day was too far advanced for them to do more than inspect that glorious landscape from the lookout. Somerville asked them to imagine themselves standing on Pulpit Rock, as though they owned as far as they could see. Then, when he felt that they had grown sufficiently complacent at that prospect, he said to them, "Of course, you never could own it. It's all National Park, but more importantly, land like this owns us, if you like, not the other way around. Our focus on this trip is geographical and geological — but never forget that this is Dharug/Gundungurra country, a place we may wonder at but never control, and never exploit."

"What was all that about?" said George. But the others shook their heads at him. His family-owned vast tracts of Victoria's Western District: George could not be expected to understand.

The fresh air had done its work and by nine o'clock most of the boys were wanting to be asleep. There was a small sitting area attached to one of the dormitories and four or five who needed more time to settle before sleep could overtake them sat on, soft drinks and chocolates keeping them going.

"So Somerville says that tomorrow we walk way down and then way back up," said Cec. "It'll be murder."

They were never quite sure how much of Cec was an act, carefully contrived, and so the easiest thing was just to laugh at him. He was not in the mood to let them off so quickly. "I mean, what if one of us breaks a leg in one of those canyons we saw on the film? Or takes a wrong path? What then? You could be lost in there for ever."

"Nobody gets to wander off, Cec. We'll be fine," said George.

"Roger might," said Shu.

Nobody wanted to comment about that and they took refuge in the chocolates. Eventually Shu took it up again. "I mean, if he thinks there is a shot he just has to get, he'll go anywhere."

Still there was silence. Roger had poked his head in half an hour previously and had then been abruptly called away by Mr Millane. He could not overhear them, they knew that, yet there was a reluctance to speak about him.

"He's all right," said Arty. "He takes great pictures."

"Any of you?" chimed in Bart and Arty blushed deeply.

"He and Mr Millane," began Cec, but Somerville poked his head round the door at just that moment and Cec's sentence was never finished.

"Bed, please. It's breakfast at seven, bus at eight. It's going to be a strenuous day, or morning at least."

"So long as you carry me back up, sir," said Bart as they rose from their comfortable lounging.

"You won't need me, Bart. If the feral cats down there get after you, you'll run as you've never run before."

The teacher stared grimly at the boys, wished them pleasant dreams, and left them to it. Bart felt sick.

III

The arrangement for Monday was that Fred Jones would take them all to the carpark above Wentworth Falls, leave them there at eight thirty and then have the bus at the Conservation Hut café, at the top of the Valley of the Waters, by half past twelve. There would be a restoring lunch in the café and an afternoon nursing sore muscles and poring over the fieldwork assignments. Fred, who might otherwise have had most of the morning to himself, decided to accompany the group as far as the crossing of the waterfall and then return to the bus. The others would follow the track for another kilometre or two and then make the strenuous ascent to the Conservation Hut. Everyone was to have water, muesli bars, fruit — whatever they thought best — and were instructed most fiercely to leave no trace of their having been there, beyond a footprint, and that only if they must!

They were a jolly bunch in the carpark, because they did not know what lay before them. There was the delight, the wonder of the view out to Mount Solitary, but most of the boys treated the view as a distant picture, not as somewhere they might actually go. They took photos with their phones and hoped that Somerville had been joking when he had warned them that actual reception down in the valley would be dodgy and not to rely on it.

"I'm told it evaporates almost as soon as one leaves to the top of the escarpment," he had said, with just a touch of malicious glee.

For many of them, the notion that those connections might evaporate was appalling.

They had all checked daypacks and were moving off when Shu saw Roger gazing into the lower carpark.

"Not that way, Roger. Over here," he called, but Roger stayed as he was, concentrating on… nothing, as far as Shu could see. "Was it a photo op that suddenly disappeared?"

"You could say that," said Roger. "Or I could have been mistaken." It was unusual to see him uncertain. He checked that his precious camera was comfortably settled and protected, but still ready for immediate action, and then joined Shu.

"Mistaken? About what?"

"I just… never mind, Shu. A trick of the light."

Roger was often found considering the state of the light. "You should be a cricket umpire," Shu had once said, "with one of those neat little light meters," but Roger had replied that in England, cricket umpires needed to be a bit more elastic about light conditions than in Australia.

"Otherwise, we'd never play at all," he had joked. For the moment, he contented himself with another glance into the lower carpark and shrugged. They joined the others.

The track to the top of the falls is easy but the view from the stepping stones is extraordinary — inspiring! Look back up and there is a pool and bush; look down and there is space, lots of space.

"Roger — and others," said Dawson, "you stay absolutely this side of the railing. The rocks are slippery out there. Every year there are…"

He saw no need to elaborate.

"You mean it's a long way to fall," came from one of the boys.

"And in a few minutes, you'll see how little there would be to break your fall — just nice hard rock."

"Look around you," said Guy Somerville. "Get a sense of the rock formations and the evidence of weathering. Now, for the sections that are steps, single file, please. And give way to any people you meet coming up."

They were moving off again when Guy felt a tap on his shoulder. It was Matron.

"Can I come only a little way, Guy, and then come back with Fred? Now that I look at it, I feel that I'm not up to this. I'm a bit fatigued already."

He looked at her with warmth and respect.

"Of course. I'm sorry none of us thought of it. Let Felicity know and you work it out with Fred."

I would have done it once, Matron thought. Guy's a nice man, but he has no idea that we can't all be like him. She found Fred and then checked that Bill Dawson had the first aid pack. She would walk with the boys for maybe ten minutes and then wait for Fred at the top of the falls. Maybe the two of them could find a pleasant morning tea spot. If the tea was good, she felt she could just about manage an hour or so of the somewhat vacuous chatter of Fred Jones.

By this time, the students had moved on and were strung out over a couple of hundred metres on the narrow pathway. They descended via steps cut into the rock, across narrow ledges under the rocky overhangs and sometimes through patches of bush that felt more like sudden eruptions of rainforest. Dawson and Somerville were delighted at the rapidity of the changes.

Near the back of the group, Roger joined Shu and Arty at a point where a sandstone ledge broadened out, just a bit.

"At the waterfall? Let's make it today. Come on, guys, show some spirit."

"It won't work, not in a group like this," said Shu. Arty blushed.

"Tomorrow, then. Somerville tells me there's a large pool that is the turning point of tomorrow's walk. We have to have this last one. Come on, Arty, you know it will be fun."

"We'll see," was all Arty would give.

They tramped on, feeling it in their calves as they descended on the steep and uneven steps. Before very long, they were in a densely wooded section and could hear the water. They emerged to find, or so it seemed, that the falls were virtually on top of them.

Those who had already gazed in awe were having drinks and snacks. Roger, Arty and Shu became the gazers.

"Too many people," muttered Arty and he dropped his pack to get at the food. He sat on a rock as he munched, absorbed in the colours of the spray, the solidity of the rocks that were, nevertheless, being remorselessly worn away, and the small trees that found a foothold in even the tiniest crevices.

"It's superb, isn't it?" Bill Dawson said, having sat on an adjacent rock. He saw the shining delight in the boy and wanted to encourage it. "The kind of place we want to keep like this for ever."

"I know. But it's changing all the time, isn't it? And some of these trails could wash away. Or what about a fire?"

"That's a huge danger," said Dawson. "And they can start in really inaccessible spots, impossible to get at until it's almost too late."

"But they would make for a superb photo," said Roger, who had finished eating and stood next to Arty.

"Not if you were caught in it, mate," said Dawson, who felt a strong dislike for the accomplished and over-confident young Englishman. He moved abruptly away and joined Somerville. Together they urged the group to get moving. Somerville took the lead and said that he would halt them again at the start of the ascent. Jones went to join Matron. Dawson took up a position in the middle of the group — the peloton, he joked to himself — and Madigan remained in the rear, the role of the sweeper, an easy role on this fairly flat section before the climb.

Her only task, she discovered, lay in constantly urging Roger to keep with the group. His eagerness to photograph the bush, or the glimpses of escarpment, or even the backs of those disappearing round the next bend caused her increasing frustration.

"But the play of light, the way the shadows work," he would say to her, unwilling to accept that such statements might not, in themselves, be any justification for holding up the main group.

"Yes, Roger. We must not be tailed off in this way. You have enough now, surely."

"I will never have enough," but it seemed to be said to himself, not to her. He smiled engagingly at the much older woman and then, judging that he had better not stretch the friendship, such as it was, any further, he led her briskly off.

The ascent was indeed arduous; it was both steep and constant. The students found it hard to take in, let alone marvel at, the sudden cascades and the changing vegetation when they were gasping for breath. Yes, it is the suddenness of the change, after such an easy section, that bothers them, thought Felicity, and some of these boys don't react well to change of any kind.

"We're half-way up," proclaimed Somerville, who had taken over the rear position.

"But I'm three quarters dead," moaned Arty.

"Stop for a drink, then. Have some chocolate."

"All gone, sir. I needed so much fuel at the bottom, just to get this far."

Somerville found the lad some nuts and insisted that steady if slow was much better than frequent stopping. He felt that this plodding climb out of the valley was more tortuous than if he had attempted to run it. But there had to be someone at the rear. That was a given.

They got there, although, for the last half hour, Arty Fulsom saw nothing but his own feet. The other boys cheered him as he dragged himself up the final steps and onto the Conservation Hut's deck. Bart, looking somewhat pale and wobbly, cheered the loudest. After all, Arty was not to know that he had got there only a couple of minutes before. The day was fine enough to sit outside and the pot pies, fish and chips and cakes went down most efficiently, as though in thanks for safe arrival. And Matron was grateful for good tea.

Between three and half past five, the two male teachers took their charges through the minutiae of the fieldwork assignments. Fred said that he would drive the other staff up to the Katoomba township for some exploring, as he put it. Matron announced that she would stay behind in case any boy suffered aftereffects from the morning's exercise and went to find a book. Thus it was that Fred drove Felicity Madigan and Roger Xanthius a distance they could easily have covered on foot.

"We'll meet here at five, then," Felicity said. "I'm going to find the library — Roger, your plans?"

"I'll just be in the main street — have a snack — get some photos."

"In that case, I'll leave you to it. You understand, though — just the town centre area, yes?"

I can't hold his hand, she thought, and I don't want to. It was an ugly thought. Fred said he would explore antique and second-hand shops, and they went their separate ways.

"I'm always here when I say," Roger said, smiling jovially at Felicity when she appeared on the stroke of five. He seemed to expect a compliment.

"Just as it should be," was all that she could manage. But Roger wasn't really listening to her. He seemed preoccupied with a photograph he had taken. It was merely of Katoomba Street, taken from the top of the hill, looking down at nothing but shops and some well rugged-up pedestrians. But it was one of those pedestrians that interested him, a rear view of someone ducking into a side lane, someone in army fatigues. He shook his head. Then Fred appeared, saying that the college library would be just the place for some of the splendid artefacts he had seen in the second-hand shops. "You don't fill a school library with tourist junk," Felicity almost responded but stopped herself just in time. Soon after they returned to the motel, the students were released from their assignment familiarisation. Most of them rang or messaged home — just to keep the oldies happy, they said, though there was more to it than that. Some cards appeared and Uno with at least a dozen players turned out to be a wild game. They enjoyed down time until seven, when another excellent meal was consumed.

Roger was happy to retire early. He said he had a lot to sort through. For a person determined that his record of the expedition should be comprehensive, the Uno game had been an unexpected bonus: the facial expressions and the physical connections were hilarious!

"It's all running like clockwork." beamed Guy when the last student light was turned off. "Tomorrow will be interesting in a different way, but not nearly so strenuous. Just as we planned it, eh?"

IV

Bill Dawson was the keenest weather observer in the college group and it was he who, over breakfast on Tuesday morning, announced, "Another mostly fine day but you'll need to take a coat. There are showers coming mid-afternoon; our patch of good weather might be over. Tomorrow, when we go west, it will be pretty damp. Let's make the most of today."

They grunted at him over their cereals, toast and eggs.

"I expect we'll be back to the bus from the pool around four," said Somerville, who planned so meticulously that he could never conceive of arrangements crumbling, certainly not just because of the weather. "Will we get everything done before the showers, Bill?"

"Touch and go. A bit like home in that conditions can change very suddenly. But we're never far from civilisation today. Not always within phone coverage, I suspect. But we'll be fine."

Guy rubbed his hands together in anticipation of anther efficient day. On this occasion they took packed lunches with them, ordered from Lily's Pad, a most convenient and excellent Leura establishment, and drove the short distance to the Leura cascades. The descent down the cascades and along to a lookout is as delightful a short walk as any to be found in the mountains. There is a gentle water accompaniment the whole way and they made a leisurely morning of it. It was the kind of walk in which one felt safely enclosed, perfectly secure. Roger took some cleverly comical photos of Arty on Bart's shoulders appearing to hold up a massive rock overhang; Matron enjoyed the walk to the lookout but opted out of an up-and-down loop via another vantage point; and at midday, with the sun still shining — not warmly, for it was winter, after all — she had the packed lunches and the thermoses all laid out.

"Whoever Lily is, she deserves a medal," said Arty. Nobody disagreed.

After lunch, the teachers led a review session with their students, as they wanted them to contrast the different watery environments they would see. Bill Dawson, gazing skyward, said that they had better get their second walk done, to the Pool of Siloam, while the weather lasted. A few minutes later, the bus dropped them at the Gordon Falls carpark. Fred and Matron South stayed in the bus and the group headed off. It was to be an easy walk in and then something rather more strenuous on the way out. Their route was to be a loop, via Lyrebird Dell, and then steeply straight back up the hill to the bus.

"I'd much prefer that to simply coming back the way we went in. It's no fun just repeating ourselves," said Dawson, who felt that others would always see it his way. "We'll spend some time at the pool, before the climb out, which is much shorter than yesterday's. I think we can be done by four."

It was easy walking, on a good track, through light bush and with only a few patches of steep steps. They spread out in a loose line, chatting comfortably and pointing out birds and lizards as though those things were rarities where they came from. Then, as they got closer to the Dell, the track degenerated into sloppy, muddy pools. They arrived at a small waterfall and pool ("No, this is not our destination," called out Somerville), quite deep, with one long side of it protected by steep sides from any winter sun. It seemed like rainforest underneath: the ferns were enormous, fresh and green, creating an impenetrable screen over the rock walls themselves. Anything could have been hidden in there, they thought. Bart leapt enthusiastically from rock to rock, missed his footing and sat plump in a mud puddle. He was hauled out, hardly knowing whether to complain more about the cold water or the hoots of laughter from his mates. Roger tried to photograph him but he dodged quickly away.

"Another couple of minutes and there will be a clearing and picnic place," said Somerville. "Come on, we'll make a pause there."

They crossed a tiny walkway over the stream that ran away from the waterfall and pool, and rounding a sudden corner, came upon the clearing. It was but a small green patch and the group felt irritated to find it already occupied. Three youngsters, two girls and a boy of about their own age, sat on a groundsheet surrounded by considerable debris — cans, food wrappers, books, piles of papers. They looked up, having heard the noise of the approaching group and they groaned loudly at the advent of an invasion by a school party. Such a mob was precisely what they had wanted to escape from.

Somerville, as usual, was amongst the first to emerge into the clearing and he immediately pointed the college students to one side of it.

"We won't disturb you," he said to the locals, if that's what they were. "We'll just collect here before we move on to the pool. It's not far away, is it?"

"Siloam? No, not far," muttered the boy, in a surly way, but the girls merely sniggered. One said, pointing at Bart, "Just don't fall in," and the three of them laughed. The boy may have decided to be cheery instead of surly because he raised a can in a kind of salutation, but perhaps it was in mockery, or a gesture telling them to get lost. After all, a school group would not be allowed beer.

Somerville turned and watched others arrive in the clearing.

"We'll pause a moment," he said and went over to Felicity. Some of the boys could not help staring at the locals and their sheer proximity proved too much for Arty. He ambled over.

"This looks like a good place for — what? — reading and drinking." His gaze took in the picnic table, on which were a few more books and papers, and an overhang amounting almost to a cave where there were day packs, and he thought, some sleeping bags. "It's a great place for a camp-out."

He came across as harmlessly friendly and one of the girls smiled at him.

"Two days of solid revision here is better than two weeks of it at home," she offered. "You know how it is — or perhaps you don't."

Roger joined the little group.

"I'm taking a visual record of our trip," he said. "Can I get a shot of you three?"

He was at once ready with his camera, assuming, as usual, that he could do as he wished, but the boy jumped up.

"No!" he shouted. "We're not part of your excursion, whatever it is. Leave us alone. No photos."

"It's OK, Alex," said the milder of the girls but the other turned away and made some comment, not really under her breath, in a mock pommy accent.

"Well, I'll have to settle for a general shot of the area," said Roger and he moved to one side of the little clearing. He took several quick shots all around, including, it seemed, of the cave.

"Be snappy, Roger," said Somerville, with entirely unconscious irony. "All down to the pool, now." He did not want any unpleasant interactions to blow up out of nothing. The boy and the mocking girl had retreated to the cave; the other girl watched them leave the clearing, Roger continuing to take his photos, then she turned to the others.

"It's OK now, Alex and Ginny. They've gone, even the pommy jerk with the camera. And we were going to pack up soon. Let's finish now, since we've been interrupted."

"We're on the last Maths topic," said the boy Alex. "I say we stick at it. We were nearly finished — but I want to be totally finished. And the car's only at the end of Gladstone, at Bertie's place. It's not thirty minutes' walk. We've heaps of time."

The track was narrow, muddy and slippery in places. The college group paused briefly at a spot, looking directly down at the pool, then made their way, by very steep steps, to the bottom. It was getting on for three, by which time the sun lit only the higher branches and the golden tops of the western facing rock walls, but the pool and its surrounds were becoming chill. A couple of students felt the water and drew back as though in alarm. Can one ever swim in these mountain pools? they wondered. Perhaps on the very hottest days? A few others found flat stones and skimmed them across the pool, enjoying the thud and splash as they hit the opposite wall and fell into the water. There were large stepping blocks to cross the stream as it trickled away from the pool before plunging down into impenetrable bush. From a large boulder in the middle of the opening, one could see a mass of tangled branches, some strong enough, maybe, to support a very brave climber. But it all looked disturbingly damp, cold, tangled and forbidding.

Somerville and Dawson, mindful of the time and the already rapidly falling temperature, gathered the students and pointed out useful examples of erosion, of layers in the rock, of strata in the flora as one looked up from pool level to the path by which they had arrived. Roger was taking photographs with eager abandon and proclaiming that he could envisage a three-hundred-and-sixty-degree record of such a magical place. It was three-fifteen when the word to be ready to move on was given.

"I wish we could have stayed longer, but I'm not confident of the weather," advised Somerville. "There is a good path up to the bus but it is steep steps for much of the way. So take your time," and he concluded in his usual, confident way, "and no slipping and sliding around. It's not dangerous — but don't do a Bart on me."

He and the readiest students began the ascent. He had arranged with Madigan and Dawson, who had the first aid pack, to follow in the middle of the group. On this occasion, Millane was the sweeper. In no time, the faster walkers were at the fork, and instead of turning right, back towards the Lyrebird Dell, they took the left-hand path and carefully, on an increasingly sloppy track, they headed up. Soon most of the party had cleared the fork with Millane trying, in vain it seemed, to hustle Roger and the slowest students along. They seemed to be busily engaged in getting themselves ready; in any case, they did not see the three local teenagers at the viewing point where they themselves had stopped earlier.

"We'll wait a moment," said Alex. "I don't want to have to talk to that lot again." He scowled down at them with a look of distaste. Or perhaps he was envious of something about them. If so, he could not explain such a feeling to himself. And that made him even more unwilling to come face to face with them again.

"And especially not the photographing fool," muttered Ginny, grinning happily at her own alliteration; even Fiona, who had been the approachable, chatty one, agreed. They put down their packs, stood unseen and observed. Ginny took out a folder and started to go over some notes. The other two, perhaps with very different feelings, were watching the events below. Both were anxious that the school group should leave: in Alex's case because he resented the growing antagonism that he felt towards them and he did not want his feeling to be put to the test; and Fiona because she simply wanted the camp-out to be over. They had, she supposed, studied effectively, but she was starting to wish that she had never come. It was all very awkward.

Millane was watching with some concern as all but the tail-end group disappeared up the steps. He turned angrily to Roger and told him to get a move on but Roger, and Arty and Shu for that matter, seemed unwilling to leave the pool. Bart also was with them, sitting on one of the large stones, clutching at his stomach and regretting the mammoth amounts of chocolate he had consumed. Millane tried his luck in that direction.

"Come on, Bart, the time is slipping away." Then, with even more concern, he asked, "Are you feeling all right?"

The lad had turned very pale. "I feel lousy. I'm going..." and suddenly he rushed to the edge of the bushes and vomited violently. There was nothing for it — Millane waited patiently then helped him back to the rock.

"Perhaps that will ease things for you. We have to go now, Bart, and get you back up top, where there will be more assistance. Come on."

He helped the boy up and called over his shoulder to the others, "Keep right with me, you lot. I can't have you staying here."

"We're right with you, sir," called Arty. "We're just putting the last few bits and pieces in the pack. You help Bart — we'll be with you in a minute."

Millane looked doubtful. He could not possibly leave the two students with Roger in charge, Roger who did not seem to understand the meaning of the word responsibility. However, with Bart clutching his belly and quietly retching, he felt he had to make a move. He looked up the trail, hoping to see someone who could take charge of Bart. The trail was empty. He had no choice but to get moving. With Bart, he would be advancing slowly — the others would soon catch up.

"Right behind me, then. I mean it, boys. I need to get Bart up top."

"Should we help them?" whispered Fiona, but Alex simply held a finger to his lips. They continued to watch in silence. They saw that, as soon as Millane and Bart were well on their way up the steps towards the fork, Roger, Arty and Shu went into action.

"As fast as you can," ordered Roger. "So he doesn't get suspicious and come back."

He jumped up with his camera onto the large boulder that, in flood times, would have been half covered but now seemed dry and stable. The other two ran to the edge of the pool, from where, as they thought, they could not be seen, and stripped. All naked, they draped themselves across each other on a rock by the water.

"It's freezing, Roger. Get it done!" yelled Shu but Roger had needed no encouragement.

"Just a couple more," he said, then, "All done. Get your gear on."

The other two made haste to do just that. Arty was quicker and he came and stood below Roger.

"OK, we've done it for you. Let's go."

Roger grinned down at him. "Yes, you've done it, at long last. But how, I'm wondering, can I make best use of it? There must be people you'd rather didn't see this." He patted the camera.

Arty looked horrified but Shu, who had now come up, said, "You're a bastard, Roger, I'm beginning to see that. But this is just a bit of fun. Let's go."

"Fun?" said Roger, enthusiastically swinging the camera on its leather strap. "Yes, I think Parslow will find it so much fun that he'll have a fit. I'll be gone and he'll blame Millane; I'm sure you two will figure out how to get yourselves out of the mess."

"You won't do any of this." Shu looked as though he had now seen the real truth of Roger. He tried to sneer at him, but that is much more difficult when looking from a few feet below. "You'd be in it too. I'm off — come on, Arty."

"You'll be sorry you said that," yelled Roger. Then he smiled at them and said, "But it's Millane I'm after." He had a queer look of triumph on his face, the kind of look Hamlet might have had had he possessed Roger's promptness of action. The boys turned and saw him vigorously swing the camera that contained his final revenge on Chaddlehangar as he prepared to jump down from the boulder. Almost deliriously, he swung it again. I can do as I please, he thought as he felt the weight of the camera through its strap. Then, somehow, in an excess of proud achievement, he lost touch with the strap, and as his precious device flew into the air, a horrified Roger made to leap after it. He slipped as he jumped and Shu and Arty saw him crash awkwardly next to the nearest of the stepping stones and then fall backwards, so that his head hit the corner of the stone. He reached out for the camera, which had landed safely enough on sandy grit, but as he tried to stand, he let out a howl of pain. Arty and Shu looked on in stunned amazement.

"My bloody ankle! What have I done to it?"

"You're an idiot, Roger," said Shu, coming cautiously back across to him. "Just get up and let's get out of here."

"But I can't, I tell you. My ankle is killing me. And my head is ringing." He touched the back of his head and his hand came away to show a small amount of blood. "What have I done?"

The bold, cunning rebel was totally undone.

"Run up the path, boys. Tell Millane — he can't have got far with Bart — tell him I need help." He made as though to clutch his ankle, then to reach out for the camera, but he could manage neither and fell back in despair.

Alex, Ginny and Fiona saw two boys head up the path as fast as they could, Shu quickly outdistancing his friend. They looked down at Roger, who lay against the boulder, eyes closed, clenching his teeth in agony.

"Nasty bastard," muttered Alex. "He deserves all he gets."

Fiona stared at him. "We can't just leave him like that."

"Oh yes, we can. Come on — we have to go that way. But I'm not getting involved."

They walked across to the fork and turned down to the pool. In only a minute they were walking past, on the other side, as it were, but Roger must have heard the scrunch of their feet. He groaned and pointed to his leg.

"I've done something," he got out. "You haven't anything for the pain, have you?"

Alex forgot his resolution to stay uninvolved and spoke with derision.

"No, we've drunk all that." He paused. He did not understand his own fierce antipathy to Roger but something in him made him anxious to score a victory in front of his two companions.

"We saw it all from up there. And heard it all — you were going to blackmail them, weren't you? And one of the teachers, too? I'd hate to have you as one of my 'mates'."

"Come on," Ginny hissed at him. "You said no getting involved."

"But he's seen us here now," said Fiona. "We are involved."

The three moved away a little.

"We have to do something for him," said Fiona, though she sounded very uncertain.

"Why?" exploded Alex. They looked back and saw that Roger was quiet, his eyes glazed, just flickering, as though all he could think of was the pain in his ankle. "The others won't be long, I suppose. They'll bring help."

Then his eye fell on the camera, the strap just out of Roger's reach. He walked towards it.

"But I reckon we can do something for the other poor sods," he said, and to the girls' astonishment he picked up the camera, scrambled up on to the boulder and hurled it as hard as he could down the creek. He heard a satisfying crash and turned to see the girls staring at him. He looked down at Roger again.

"He's out to it now. Come on, let's go."

"I think we should…" but Alex was having none of it.

"Packs on. He's only got a busted ankle, and we can't do anything about that."

"I don't like it," said Fiona. She made as though to move towards Roger but stopped at a fierce glare from Alex.

"Neither do I," came from Ginny as she settled her pack. "The guy's a jerk. We should have stayed right out of it." She led the way, totally indifferent to the fallen Englishman.

"I'm right with you," said Alex. He could not have explained his actions, much less his feelings, but now he was ashamed of what he had done. He had betrayed strong feeling in a way he would normally scorn. Now he just wanted to be gone. Even Fiona could do nothing but make a hasty retreat. They all went to the other side of the clearing. Fiona looked briefly back at the inert Roger and then hastened after the other two as they disappeared up the track.

V

Bart Springside was making only slow progress. He needed to stop and retch every couple of minutes, and when he was on the move, his legs were shaking and his colour was drifting sharply between red (retching) and pitifully pale. He was most unwell, yet Millane had little option but to urge him to press on, with promises of Matron, medicine and cosy care. His tactic was working, but it was a tedious business.

Then there was another worry. He and Bart had been gone from the pool for ten minutes, but there was still no sign of Arty, Shu and Roger. Why not? Photographs, he supposed, but surely there was a limit, even for Roger. His instructions had been blunt. If it were not for Bart's trouble, he would have stayed — should have stayed, others would say — but Bart had been quite overcome with the vomiting. If a smart walker would make the ascent in fifteen minutes, it was going to take him, half supporting Bart, at least three times that long. By that time, there would be worry at the carpark, understandably. It was all such a mess. Perhaps the delay would cause them to send out reinforcements — and with this encouraging thought, he plodded on, half supporting and always urging Bart, step by weary step.

Perhaps five minutes later, when he hoped he might be halfway up, he heard noisy running behind him. He turned and was immediately anxious — why only Shu? But yes, now he could see Arty, a good way behind.

"What's happened? Where's Roger?" he blurted out.

Shu panted up to him.

"Sir, Roger's hurt. We think it's his ankle, broken or very badly sprained, but he can't walk on it."

"Oh hell!" exclaimed Millane. What now? he thought. He sat Bart down on a log — just attend to one thing at a time! — and asked for more explanation.

"He was up on that boulder, you know, the big one, last photo and all," and here he cast an uneasy glance at a panting Arty, "and he went to jump off it and slipped. We think he must have hurt his head too, but he was talking OK, he just couldn't get up."

The boy paused and looked once more at his fellow student. Millane was half aware that there was more to what had happened but he was too busy assessing options to think it through. He needed an instant decision. But first, he asked, "So he's there by himself, is he? One of you should have stayed. You would have been quicker by yourself, Shu." He checked his phone — still no reception.

Arty looked desperate — he could not have stayed alone with Roger, not after what had been said and done.

"We can't help that now," continued Millane, deeply disturbed that his Roger minding seemed so spectacularly to have failed. "So I'll head straight back. Arty, you go up slowly with Bart. Shu, you race up as fast as you can, give the news and say we'll need some help. Possibly medics, ambulance — they can decide. But don't stay — come on straight back. Downhill's quick, you'll only be ten minutes behind me. The two of us together may be able to help Roger. And bring Mr Dawson and the medical kit. OK?"

It was rapid, but definite and efficient. The boys nodded.

"Then get going," and he saw Shu head up at a gallop, the other two at a stagger. He turned and hurried downwards.

Shu delivered his news to a horrified group. But all their questions took up time, precious time. Eventually, Shu and Mr Dawson set off, leaping, they felt, down the steps. It must have been fifteen, maybe nearly twenty minutes since he had left Millane that Shu saw him again, sitting with his head in his hands beside an apparently still unconscious Roger Xanthius. Millane heard them as they came down the last slippery section below the fork and he came very slowly across the clearing towards them. He looked strangely, despairingly, at the puffing Dawson and then at the boy. One was too agitated, and the other too exhausted, to read his expression, but they heard him clearly enough.

"You told me about the ankle and the head. You didn't tell me he was dead."

VI

Back at the carpark, tempers were disturbed, though things had not gone so far as panic. On the one hand, they knew so very little, and there was too much to do. Bart Springside was immediately handed over to the care of Matron South who, for the time being, could do little more than lie him down across the rear seat of the bus and keep a bucket handy. Once there had been no vomiting for half an hour, she felt more at ease and the boy fell into a light doze. To maintain that state for Bart, the others were kept outside in the growing gloom and chill, but by half past four, and in vindication of Mr Dawson's prognosis, steady misty showers descended and there was no other shelter: into the bus they crammed.

Felicity Madigan, as the senior staff member present, was dealing with the necessary services. Just as the showers swept in, causing once bright cliffs to disappear from view and inducing in all of them intense worry about conditions for poor Roger down below, the ambulance arrived and two calm but purposeful paramedics got out. Madigan, a coat over her shoulders, went to meet them.

"I am very relieved that you are here. I don't exactly know what you'll find down at the pool. As I understand it, a young man has an injured ankle, possibly a head wound, and he can't move. There are two teachers and one student there with him."

She had spoken clearly but very rapidly, as though she had rehearsed what she took to be the essential information. One of the medics raised a hand, while the other strapped on a hefty backpack.

"Steady there," said the shorter, darker one, presumably the senior partner. "Who is injured? Do we know how? Are we sure he can't move by himself?"

Felicity looked exasperated. "We don't know much. We are told he can't move, that he hurt his leg and head jumping off a boulder. He slipped as he jumped. He may need specialist help getting up that steep track. I just don't know."

The senior ambo, James, looked at his partner, Helmer, and got a nod. He turned back to Felicity.

"We know the Pool of Siloam well enough. But we need to take one of your party with us, just to be sure we are heading to exactly the right spot. People who are new to the area — and that's you, isn't it? — get confused, you know and… this late, and in this weather… we need to be sure."

Felicity slowly took this in. "At least the information that the boy is right at the pool seemed clear and certain," she said, then she beckoned to Arty to come out of the bus. "I need you to make another trip down, Arty. Confirm for these men exactly where Roger is. And it might help him to see a friend."

Arty blanched. "Shu is there... I really don't... I can't... I mean, it's the coming back up that will kill me." There was no way he was going to face Roger again, not so soon, not right now.

Felicity stared at him, shocked. She had expected that he would want to be with Roger. Now she found it to be just the opposite. His reluctance had something to do with Roger, she felt, not with the strenuous walk. An unexpected feeling of doom stole over her. So whom to send? Fred? No use, because he would be totally new to the track. Guy? — she would like another teacher up here, but he was fit enough. And if her intuition of disaster was correct, she didn't want another student down there anyway. She wondered what on earth had gone on.

Within a minute, Guy and the two ambulance men had gone off down the trail. How can they be so calm, wondered Felicity, and then realised that that was part of their job. She glanced in at Matron: there was another calm one, with her patient totally under control. And Fred? — nothing ruffled him. He could meet any unexpected incident with simple determination to plug on. The sight of such people was reassuring. She relaxed.

Only a few minutes later, however, her feeling of reprieve crumbled. She noticed Guy Somerville, alone, come out of the mouth of the trail, and instead of coming to the bus and out of the dismal gloom, he stood some twenty metres away and appeared to beckon to her. With great apprehension, she left the bus. Several students, looking up, noticed Somerville and registered a problem. By the time Felicity came up to her colleague, therefore, half of the students were either looking out the door of the bus or peering through its windows. It was just light enough for Felicity to see him clearly. She received a shock.

"It's worse than we thought, Guy?" She asked it breathlessly.

"Triple zero again, Felicity. But this time the police. The medics insist on it, straight away. "

She could not put the pieces together.

"They've gone on down with Shu — he met us only five minutes down the path. According to him, Felicity, Roger is dead."

Such a statement can sometimes be made gently and after suitable preparation. Not this time. Felicity felt that she could not take it in.

"We will say nothing to the group," he continued, "until we know for sure. But please call for police assistance. For the moment, we will say that it is a National Parks requirement when there is a bad injury and that we didn't know that before."

He stopped and looked more closely at her.

"I'm sorry, Felicity, more than I can say. You ring. I'll make my announcement in the bus."

Trembling, she reached for her phone.

VII

The hefty backpack contained, among other things, a strong nylon stretcher fitted to a structure made of tent poles, collapsible but very strong once assembled. James went to talk to the two men he found at the pool, while Helmer put the stretcher together. He saw the tall boy on the ground and groaned at the likely weight.

"Thank God you're here. I just can't understand it," blurted out Dennis Millane. "I heard he was hurt, jumping off that boulder behind him, but I didn't…"

He could not go on. James bent to the young man on the ground.

"One of your students, then?" he said as he quietly confirmed to himself that he was dealing with a dead body.

"No," came in Dawson. "A young man, out of school, doing a kind of work experience out here. From England," he added and wondered why he had done so. Maybe all the facts were important, somehow.

"And this young man," said James, gesturing at Shu. "He saw what happened?"

Shu came hesitantly forward. He was barely able to speak. His life, difficult as it might at times have felt to him, had given him no signposts to help him navigate through this kind of misery and confusion.

"He'd taken a photo. He jumped off but slipped." Shu stared up at the boulder — reliving it? Hoping it would all turn out differently if he played it through in his mind once again?

"Go on, boy," said James. "Gently as you like, but we have to know."

"So, he slipped." Shu was trying to gather the threads in his mind but they were as slippery as the rock had been for Roger. "He fell. Yelled. We were just over there," and he pointed to the first of the steps out of the pool area, "and he yelled that he couldn't get up and had cracked his head."

Then it all came in a rush.

"And yes, his head had blood, but he was talking to us, he was OK except for the ankle, and he sent us for help because he couldn't get up. He said it was just the ankle, but he was OK." The words now faded slowly away. "He was OK."

Meanwhile, Helmer had set the stretcher down and was examining Roger's body, very tentatively.

"It's a very nasty gash," he said. "Very nasty — quite a lot of blood."

He made no comment, just let the words sit there. Shu was suddenly terrified.

"Just a bump," he cried. "It was only the leg, the ankle, that was the problem."

The two ambos looked at each other. It was nearly dark by now and Helmer went to the pack, pulling out two huge torches. Their light made everything eerie. Against rock walls they threw shadows that seemed to have a life of their own, and in Shu's state of terror, they accused him — of what, he didn't know.

"For the moment," said James, "we wait for the police. They won't be long."

"But, really," said Millane, "for an accident like this? Is that necessary?"

"Yes, sir, it is," came the blunt reply. "I'm sorry to keep you here in these conditions, but it has to be. It's cold, and it's going to get colder, but it won't be long until they are here and we can tidy all this up."

Quite what manner of tidying he meant was not clear. The two teachers looked at each other in dismay. Shu was shivering violently, and it wasn't from the cold.

"He said he was OK. It was the leg — it was only the leg."

VIII

For Felicity Madigan, as she said afterwards to Headmaster Parslow, it was the longest afternoon and evening of her life. To be forced to come to terms with, to deal with a death in one's group constitutes the most feared nightmare in the mind of any school teacher. That it wasn't actually one of her students was no consolation, and as the evening wore on, it became clear to her that two who were her students were not being regarded as mere bystanders to an unfortunate accident. There was suspicion, and its implications terrified her. In addition, Dennis Millane had completely gone to pieces and whether it was because he had failed in his responsibilities by not being the last to leave the pool or because he had failed to protect one who had been put particularly under his care, she could not tell. It was probably both of those things. If he had had the means to drink himself into a stupor, he would have done so; lacking such means, he simply sat, a nervous, wide-eyed, gibbering mess.

It was not as though Felicity were under scrutiny herself, not in any real way. Her movements, and in fact, the movements of almost all the party could be established with absolute certainty. But there were murky areas, for which information, partial as it was, came to her through Bill Dawson and through the interviews undertaken by Sergeant Maddie Provis of the Katoomba police. She had, of course, been present at those interviews and now tried to form a coherent picture, to clear away at least some of the murk.

Provis and a junior constable, Aaron Young, had arrived at the pool a little before five o'clock. By then it was quite dark in the pool surrounds, with drizzling rain, low cloud and no sense of the sky above or even of the tops of the rock faces. Provis had, it seemed, gone straight to the ambulance men to confirm the situation; Young's task had been, torch in hand, to check exactly who was there and to make a list of names. He did not speak conversationally to anyone — he simply made his list of names. Then Provis had called Millane and Dawson to her and moved them to one side of the clearing.

"Is one of you in charge down here? I have spoken briefly to those up top."

The two teachers looked uncertainly at each other.

"I think I can answer your questions." Dawson gave his name. "Dennis Millane is a teacher on exchange from England — but I have more to do with this excursion." He paused. "I take it there is no doubt…"

"Oh, sir," said Provis, "would our medical people have been sitting idle if there was a doubt?" Then she must have taken pity on him. "I understand your position. There has been a death in your party. So far, I have been given to understand that we are dealing with a tragic accident. But there appears to be some confusion over what happened — a leg injury? A head injury? Both, it seems. We just need to establish that."

She looked at him expectantly. Dawson turned to his fellow teacher.

"Dennis, fill in bits as necessary." But Millane had become mute with anxiety and Dawson went on.

"As I understand it, the lad who died, Roger, and two of our boys, were the last to be here. Dennis…"

"Just the three boys, then? No teacher with them?" Her tone was meant to register some mystification at this.

"Well, you see, Dennis had taken a sick boy on ahead a little, to help him up the track." Dawson wondered if that was enough. "He had been vomiting. He had to be got moving straight away. Is that right, Dennis?"

Millane managed a nod.

"You explain the next bit, Dennis. You were there." Millane seemed to make a massive effort.

"The boy Bart and I were some way up the track, half-way, maybe not even that, when Shu and Arty rushed up to tell me of Roger's accident, and that he couldn't move." He took a deep breath. "I came back here. Arty was to help Bart and Shu was told to race to the top as fast as he could and ask for assistance. Ambulance, or whatever." He gasped. Provis had the sense not to push him. "I got here, and after a while Bill and Shu, the boy over there, came back."

"And when you got here, you found… what?" She was determined not to lead him.

Millane could not look up at her.

"Just Roger." He gasped for breath. "I went over to ask him how he was managing. But… but… And then I did the best I could with CPR… but…"

"Was there any sign of anyone else?"

He all but collapsed onto one of the stepping stones. It was all he could do to shake his head.

"Now, I need you to try hard here, Mr Millane. Tell me how much time passed between the boys leaving this — Roger — and your return. For how long must he have been alone?"

He looked up and answered simply, "They would have run hard. We spoke for a couple of minutes." Millane sank his head in his hands again and murmured, "Ten, twelve minutes. Surely not more than fifteen."

Provis turned back to Dawson.

"And then you and the boy got here after another…? How long?"

Dawson calculated rapidly.

"Shu ran up, we hurtled back down — all up, another fifteen minutes, maybe."

As he related all this to Felicity later, he expressed his surprise, and concern, about Provis's determination to establish a time sequence. Did it mean that quicker action might have saved Roger? But how? They had sent for help as quickly as they could.

The next arrival at the pool, Dawson went on to explain, was a doctor accompanied by another policeman. The doctor's official role was to say what everyone already knew, but aided by an array of torches, he made a more extensive examination of Roger's body than a mere pronouncement of death required. He looked carefully at the head wound, the ankle and the leg and then instructed the ambos to use their stretcher and begin what would be a very tricky ascent, in the dark and on a now muddy track. Dawson heard him say to Provis, "Come and see me in the morning, say about ten; or I can send a message," and then he was seen no more. Provis asked the three members of the college to sit on the large stones that crossed the clearing from one side to the other.

"I don't want to talk to you here, in the dark, under these conditions. But I will need to get clear statements from each of you — tonight. Constable, bring up the rear with your torch; I'll lead with mine. Be very careful in the dark."

They trudged up, making frequent stops on account of Millane who seemed to need to look back in the direction of the pool every few steps, until he could see it no more. Sergeant Provis did not urge him on, because, Dawson supposed, she did not wish to catch up with the stretcher party. It seemed like an hour before they came out into the Gordon Falls reserve and saw the bus. The ambulance must already have gone: James and Helmer had done an heroic job under the conditions. Now there was only the bus, and only Fred Jones and Felicity Madigan with it.

"Guy and Matron have the students back at the motel," she had said to him. "Come on — fill me in as we go."

But Sergeant Provis intervened.

"I'll see you at the motel very shortly. I've already told your staff, and the boy, that I will need statements tonight."

"Surely that's not necessary? We will be dealing with shock and grief tonight. Some other time, please."

"I'm afraid not." The sergeant was adamant. "It is important that everything is quite clear."

"Is anything of importance unclear?"

Sergeant Provis did not give a direct answer.

"I'll ring Colleen at the motel — I know her well — and arrange a discreet room. But it must be tonight."

At that they had parted and Felicity was left to contemplate the horror of a night's questioning and explaining. Anyone who has read, or watched, even a few detective stories, knows how unsettling that can be. And Felicity was a secret fan.

She was certainly not a fan of Sergeant Provis by the time the evening was done. The questioning had been calm but insistent, and by not implying anything in particular, it had left everything up in the air. By the time Felicity had the lights off in the student rooms and could sit back with Bill Dawson and Matron, she felt as though she had been grilled, turned over, and grilled again. She was significantly overdone. Matron made tea, found a packet of chocolate biscuits and sat quietly on one side.

"Is Dennis out to it, then?" Felicity asked Dawson.

"Looks like it. Poor man. For this to happen, just before he leaves. He's fallen apart. When I saw him in his bed, he was mumbling to himself about telling the family of Roger back in the UK." He paused briefly. "I can't see him coping with what's left of our trip."

"If there is a 'what's left'," commented Felicity. At that point Guy Somerville came in to report that all seemed quiet but that Fred Jones had offered to sit near the boys' rooms as a calming presence should one be necessary.

"Fair enough, I suppose," said a dubious Felicity. "It's hard to predict how Shu and Arty will react to all this. Shu particularly."

She raised an eyebrow at her colleagues, asking for a comment, or perhaps checking that her own observations were shared by the others. But they remained silent.

"OK," she said. "Let's see where we are at and what is possible for tomorrow. Firstly, I have spoken to Allan Parslow, twice in fact, and he is to be the link to Chaddlehangar and the family. He will also be in touch with all our families, though the boys have all made contact themselves by now. Still, Allan might have something to say in the morning. The police have spoken to us all — ourselves privately, but to the students with either me or you, Guy, sitting in. Given the way they are behaving, I am not at all clear how we can contemplate our westward excursion tomorrow. Yes?"

Bill Dawson looked crestfallen but Guy had no doubts.

"Absolutely. There is going to be more questioning tomorrow, especially of Dennis and the two boys. We can't go out and leave them to face it. We could, I suppose, make a day of assignment work, couldn't we, Bill?"

His colleague only stared gloomily at him. Somerville went on.

"And the weather is going to be awful. There really is no alternative." He turned to Felicity. "I'm not sure Sergeant Provis would let us all go in any case. And we must keep the whole group together."

"I'll announce at breakfast," said Felicity, "so that it is *our* decision. It is for the best, Bill."

Dawson simply shook his head, but at what remained unclear. For the first time, Matron entered the conversation.

"It would be good to distract them. I'm not disagreeing, not at all, but once the day's program becomes clear, get Fred to run some of them up to town, maybe in groups. Or for lunch, since we won't be taking it out with us. You don't want them to feel imprisoned."

She sat back, feeling that perhaps her comments were not acceptable in the same way tea and biscuits were. The others nodded, but she felt that her comments had hardly been registered. She retreated.

"There will be a lot of waiting around, I fear," said Felicity. "We'll just have to take it as it comes." She took a deep breath. "Look, our charge is to look after our fifteen students. I dare say we don't quite know what we feel, or ought to feel, about Roger" (Guy gave her a sudden, sharp look) "but our boys come first now. And I am deeply concerned for two of them. An accident has somehow turned into a mysterious death and they have been questioned as though their part in this mystery needs explanation. So let's make tomorrow as calm and practical and useful as we can. All agreed?"

They seemed to be. Matron began to gather up the mugs and plates. Bill Dawson muttered, "Mystery indeed."

"What do you mean by that?" snapped Felicity.

He looked across at Somerville. "I know it was dark, and I didn't have long. But I did check Roger's things and then scout about." He paused, as though asking them to fill the obvious gap. "Well?" and he held out one hand as though to drag an answer from them. "Why is it that there was no sign of his famous camera?"

There was an "Oh!" from Matron but she was already half-way out the door. Felicity sat rigid. Somerville said, "Has anyone told the police that?"

"If one of us hasn't," said Dawson, and got negatives from the others, "then that's another part of tomorrow we hadn't planned on."

Felicity came out of her trance.

"It surely is," she said. "Good night to us all."

But long after Matron's breathing indicated the relief of sleep, Felicity was uncomfortably awake. It was not because of anxiety about the day just finished, and it was not from sorrow. It was distress right enough, arising from doubts she was unable to suppress about what had happened at that pool and fear of what the next day might bring.

IX

One thing it brought was Detective Inspector Esson.

At the end of her long evening of interviews, Maddie Provis had felt some real degree of uncertainty about how to proceed. She knew that the facts as she had been given them permitted an easy and straightforward explanation: death by most unfortunate accident. Yet she felt uncomfortable. There was confusion over the leg or the head; there was the doctor's brief comment that, as far as he could see, there were two head wounds; then the time — quarter of an hour? — during which the English lad lay there alone. Perhaps most of all there was the behaviour of the teacher on exchange, alone with a body — or perhaps with someone still alive. She needed help to sort it all out. Her interviews had also alerted her to another matter requiring follow-up, namely, the other teenagers in the vicinity. It sounded as though they had behaved strangely and it was possible that they knew something. She had worked with Craig Esson before, so she had phoned down to Springwood to see if he was available. "Expect me first thing in the morning," he had told her.

Esson was a small, dark-haired, slightly pudgy man of forty or thereabouts. A resident of Leura, he had until recently worked at Katoomba, until a promotion saw him based at Springwood and now, supposedly, available for the entire Blue Mountains area. He was regarded by his superiors as reliable, a little unconventional, about as likely, or unlikely, as anyone else to solve a crime. But there was a great deal more to him than that. Maddie had liked working with him because he loved to summarise, out loud and frequently, so that she found him easy to follow. Well, mostly easy — he had the very odd tendency to burst into German for no apparent reason. She had got used to the occasional '*Jawohl*', but sometimes it was much worse than that. Still, if he had to have a peculiarity, it was a harmless one.

Esson had no family in the local area. His parents and his one sibling, a sister, lived further north, in a suburb of Newcastle, but when he had completed his training, he had been posted to Katoomba and had fallen in love with the area. The townships, larger and smaller, had each their own character, a real individuality. He loved Leura, particularly his small cottage tucked into a back street but within easy walking distance of the village centre. He was fond of Wentworth Falls, a realistic sort of place, not as perfectly twee as Leura, but with its own rugged splendour, and it was home to Schwarz Patisserie, and he could not go past something as Germanic as that! If he needed to hide for a day,

Bullaburra was the place of choice, a village so gently asleep that motorists even tried to drive quietly for the few seconds they were in its environs. Or Mount Victoria, or Bell — there were many places that allowed one to disappear for, say, half a day in order to have a good think. And if half a day was not available, there was Lily's Pad, with fine coffee and satisfying food only a couple of streets from home. Why would one ever want to leave the mountains?

He had left the upper mountains, however, the only part of the whole district that is, in locals' minds, true mountains, had left it at least as far as his daily job went. He had been encouraged to apply for a position that entailed regional oversight — was it really that they wanted to move him on from Katoomba? — and the opportunity had, on the whole, come at a good time. He had been still trying to put behind him a most unpleasant case, one involving improper behaviour in a sporting club. He had hated sifting through the various statements, conducting interviews with people who, he knew, were intent on misleading him. He had brought the case to a reasonable conclusion but there had been little satisfaction in reaching that point. He had been left with a strong sense that betrayal of trust had been the real issue, and that was a problem that would be hopelessly difficult to repair in the hearts and minds of the victims. And nearly everyone involved was a victim, one way or another. So he had moved his base of operations, trying to wash away the stain of that troubling case, while he still lived in the area he loved. To tell the truth, he missed the Katoomba gang.

One he missed was Maddie Provis. He had seen her work her way through the ranks, as it were, and become a well-respected Detective Sergeant, a person on her way to higher honours, he felt sure, so long as decency and keen perception were the qualities that would be needed for such honours. She was a local born and bred, with a good knowledge of both the townships and the various walks, simple or immensely challenging, that led out from them. She had worked with Esson on various cases, including the sporting club one, and though she could still be a little literal in jumping to conclusions, he had great faith in her good sense. He wondered how much she had sensed of his unease, the way in which, in the sporting club case, he had seemed to need to burst out at the duplicity of several of the interviewees. She had almost moved to restrain him once or twice but had thought better of it. It was hard to restrain one's superior. And she had put up splendidly with his odd bursts of German. Did she sense that they came at moments when insight was tantalisingly close? Anyway, it would be good to work with her again.

"O'Loughlin was quite happy to send me up here for a day or two." Esson felt that the Springwood Superintendent was not his greatest fan. "I know the area. *Gut, ja?*" He grinned impishly at her. He had had a perfectly good night's sleep, and over coffee and croissants at seven in the morning, he felt in the mood for something interesting. She summarised what she knew as best she could; perhaps her account was coloured by the fact that she had not had such a restful night.

"I see," he responded. "So we have fifteen minutes when the poor sod is alone, and then fifteen minutes of only the teacher from England. Of course, anything could have happened when the kid was supposedly alone. There is that group of three youngsters lurking somewhere on the fringe, though I know they may be totally uninvolved, and who knows who else was around. It's school holidays, after all. And in all that, we are not sure exactly when he died. So, first thing this morning, set others to tracking down the mysterious three. You will take me to the pool and then, maybe by nine, to the motel. *Richtig*! They won't like it but it will be interviews all over again." He shoved the last bit of croissant into his mouth, began to say *'wunderbar'* but nearly choked as he swallowed and almost dragged her off with him. In the street, he said, "Get the other young policeman — Young, is it? — to meet us there. I want to know if anything looks different in the daylight."

They parked at the Gordon Falls reserve and found the tracks to the pool taped off, both the direct path down and the track via the Lyrebird Dell.

"There are other ways of getting in, as I recall, aren't there?" he asked Young. "Are they secure too?"

"Yes, sir," said the nervous but superbly eager constable.

"Yes, to which of my questions? Both, I hope!" Provis intervened.

"There's an entry from near the bottom of Gladstone Road and another that comes not far from Everglades. All closed off — that last one only by tape."

"Fair enough, considering when all this occurred. Well, what are we waiting for? Is there anything for me up here?"

"Steady on, sir. Just orient yourself. This is where all the coming and going started." She pointed out the two main tracks, explained how one ran just off the road and could be easily accessed from further up Gordon Road. That entrance was taped off too, she said.

"We must have very tape-conscious, law-abiding people up here," Esson said. "Wouldn't do much good down on the plains. Lead on," and they headed down the steep, direct route to the scene of yesterday's disaster. Walking swiftly, but not running and certainly taking care in the muddy patches, it took them twelve minutes.

The cloud was low but it was not raining. At still not eight o'clock on a winter's morning, the pool area was dim, hemmed in by a dark gloominess that clung to everything. The water looked black. The foliage dripped miserably and the huge rock from which Roger had fallen was extremely slippery now, even if it hadn't been then. Esson looked hard at the spot where the body had lain and then peered over the rock, letting his gaze follow the line of the creek. He took in the tangled undergrowth and the steep drop and decided that answers were not to be found in that direction. He turned his attention back to the dim and forbidding pool area.

"People could come here along so many paths, couldn't they," he complained. Then he tried to be brisk again. "Now, the lad was up here?" and he got an affirmative nod from Young. "And he fell. Why was he up here? Do we know?"

He looked as though he might climb the rock himself, thought better of it and looked at Sergeant Provis. "Why was he up here? He wasn't a little kid, climbing for the heck of it."

"I talked to the two college students who were here with him, and…"

"The three of them, wasn't it? By themselves?"

"…and they say he was just larking about. They thought it was just him mucking around while they packed up."

"I don't think that's very…" He thought for a moment, muttered "*sehr interessant*" to himself and addressed Provis again.

"I can see why you felt a little uneasy. As you say, an accident is still a possible reading of it, but… packing up, the others, were they? But what was he up to?"

Provis decided to risk it.

"When you interview them, sir, the two boys, but others too, you may find that their attitude to Roger was, to say the least, ambiguous."

"*Ach so*," was all he would comment.

He let Mrs Madigan and Mr Somerville spend fifteen minutes filling him in, as they saw it. It was plainly established that neither of them had any part in Roger's death, but they felt that, as senior representatives of the college, they had to lead the way. They told him nothing new, probably because they told him only what they assumed he already knew.

Then he asked, "Tell me, Mrs Madigan, how did the other boys get on with this Roger fellow? Saw him as an outsider maybe?"

"Yes, to some extent that would be true." She was determined to play it very straight. "He had only been with us six months. They saw him as one who liked to push the boundaries, liked to have a lot of fun, but sometimes for him the real fun was in the risk involved. My colleagues will agree with me — he was the kind of young man you had to keep an eye on."

She had played it too honestly.

"But you didn't, did you? No staff member was keeping an eye on him when he died. How was that possible?"

"Circumstances, Mr Esson. You know that. Mr Millane felt he had to help Bart, who was vomiting, He told the three still at the pool to follow immediately. That should have been all right. Roger was older, not a student." She seemed to feel dubious about her own comments. "They didn't — not immediately, that is — and then Roger had his fall."

He let that rest — he would come back to the possible negligence of Millane later, but he would want to interview the boy Bart first — and turned to Mr Somerville.

"And you, sir — your views on Roger, please. You might form many impressions in six months. It is quite a long time in the life of a school."

"Talented in some areas, mostly reliable, wanting to push limits, as Felicity has told you." Esson was gesturing, inviting more. "So most of the boys couldn't help but like him. Some with reservations."

"I shall enjoy hearing how the boys describe those reservations. I need to…" but he glanced at his phone and hurriedly excused himself. The pathologist and his team had been told of his involvement and here was a brief statement, truncated, as a message.

Badly sp ankle. Two head wounds, one minor, one fatal. Which first?!

He stood at the door, beckoned Provis over and held the message out to her. She registered the absurdity, along with the implications for their investigation, and sighed heavily. She knew something of Dr Richardson, enough to be wary of being drawn into a verbal fencing match. She suspected that Esson secretly relished such encounters. They went back in.

"I was just about to ask…" but then he changed his mind, "…about the talents you spoke of, sir. What were they?"

"Very keen on ph…" But then Somerville stopped dead. He looked across at his senior colleague.

"Oh, don't stop there, sir. Go on!"

"It was photography, I suppose. He could take some beautiful nature shots."

Somerville had offered a simple enough statement. Was it relevant? He could not be sure. But when he had turned to Felicity and indicated a wish to interview Mr Millane, he turned back to Maddie Provis and said, loudly enough, "Bring me the kid's camera, Sergeant." He did not see Somerville wince.

Felicity Madigan spoke to him with real urgency.

"Dennis Millane has had a severe shock — and a severe reaction. He was in a bad state last night. Please make it short and simple for him, Inspector."

Esson glanced again at the message on his phone — two wounds, so not a matter of one simple fall — and then looked up at her. She was a clever and impressive woman, he sensed, trying her hardest to control what she could control.

"Thank you for the caution. I'll do what I can." But for Esson, that simply meant that he would play it as he saw fit. Then he produced a look of complete mystification on Madigan's face. "But Mr Millane can wait. I want to start with the boy Bart."

"What on earth for?" she blurted out. "He had long gone when Roger's accident occurred."

"Quite so. I just need to be sure of one or two things.

He attempted a smile which was not well received. Mrs Madigan went out to find the unsuspecting Bart. She passed Provis coming in.

"No one can locate the camera for us, sir. One of the boys, called Cec, and one of the teachers, Mr Dawson, have had a look through his things. A missing item."

Esson frowned. It had to be relevant but he could not yet see why.

"I wonder when," he began but Madigan came in at just that moment with an uncertain, but now perfectly well, Bart Springside. She sat him down and took the chair next to him. Opposite sat the two police officers. Bart fixed his eyes on Provis as, presumably, the more congenial of the two. Esson was having none of that.

"Now young man, we need to establish, very clearly, exactly what happened and when, yesterday afternoon. So I want you to be as precise as you can about times. Understood?"

The boy was very hesitant. He looked towards Provis.

"But, you see, I wasn't feeling at all well. Sick as anything, actually. I don't think I know much about times."

"Nevertheless…"

Provis sensed Esson's impatience but couldn't work out why it should be directed at this particular boy. "What you saw will still help us to fill in the picture, Bart," she said.

He seemed grateful for even that much gentle consideration.

"I began to feel unwell," he began, "just as we were told to leave the pool. It sometimes comes on me so suddenly. Doesn't it, Miss?" He looked at Mrs Madigan for support. "Just the other day, at the film they call The Edge, I had to rush out."

"Come back to yesterday," said Esson, again a little tersely, though he now realised that he would have to let this lad pace the narrative in his own way. "When you suddenly felt sick, were there many left at the pool?"

"No, not many. I was near the tail end. I wasn't looking forward to the climb out, not after the day before at Wentworth Falls. It was murder!" He almost laughed and then hid his face in embarrassment. Esson chose not to notice and ploughed on.

"So you were there, and so was Mr Millane, and…?"

"And Shu and Arty and Roger. I think that was all. But when I was throwing up into the bushes, I didn't take much notice, I have to tell you that."

For the first time, his tone was assertive, as though he now felt ready to control the interview. Esson was not going to let that happen.

"Even though you were throwing up, you heard things. What did you hear Mr Millane say to the other boys?"

"Well, I suppose… I think… well, he was trying to get them to hurry up. But Roger is always packing and repacking; he nearly always brings up the rear." He was quite unaware of his use of the present tense.

"Was he urging them, though? I have been given the impression he was more interested in you."

"He spoke to them quite sharply, sir. He said they were to follow at once."

Esson leaned a little towards the boy. "Was he really? Or was he happy for them to finish whatever they were doing?"

Madigan could stand no more.

"That's not fair, Inspector. Bart was unwell, and in any case, he should not be called on to make that kind of speculative judgement. It asks for little more than guesswork. You can ask such a thing of Mr Millane, but not of my students." She fixed him very firmly and awaited a response to her intervention.

All she got was, "As you wish. Now lad, you and Mr Millane went slowly up the path. Can you tell me how long it was before the other boys arrived to tell of the accident, or whatever it was?"

Again, Madigan was not going to let her student be the Inspector's prey, as she was beginning to see it.

"Just an estimate, Bart. You weren't looking at your watch every minute. I am sure the Inspector can understand that." As she finished speaking, she was just half aware of a quickly suppressed grin on the face of Maddie Provis.

"It wasn't just a minute or two," the boy began. He was no longer in control. "But I really don't... if it was five or twenty-five, I really don't know."

The boy wished it were over. Esson, however, was not about to be circumvented. He had no interest in Bart Springside — but something told him that he had better take a very close interest in the exact activities of Dennis Millane.

"And when the others did arrive, what did Mr Millane say to them?"

"He told Arty to help me — that was obviously right, Arty not sick was no faster than I was — and Shu was to run up top for help. He went down to where Roger was."

"Did you *see* him go straight down?"

"I wasn't looking down, I..."

"Enough, sir," came in Felicity Madigan once more. "You are implying things you have no right to, not in front of one of the boys."

She was very angry, but Esson merely sat back in his chair, and as though at a re-arranged signal, Provis took up the questioning.

"Just one more thing, if we may," she said, and her manner was quite different from Esson's. "I'd like you to tell me a bit about Roger, especially how he behaved to the rest of you students. What did you all think of him?"

The boy looked at his teacher and received a mild nod. "Yes, Bart, tell them what you felt, simply but clearly."

"But it wasn't simple, Miss, was it? He was great — funny, taking chances whenever he could, and sometimes very generous, as with his photos. But Miss," and he was still addressing his teacher, the only one in the room, as he saw it, who could possibly understand, "we still didn't quite trust him. I can't explain."

"But I need you to explain, Bart, at least a bit," said Provis. "Come on, try. We're here to listen."

"Well," and he felt that perhaps she really was listening, not like the Inspector, "for all the fun, you never quite knew whether Roger was only out to use you if he could." He turned to his teacher. "Like at the place with the dog on the tuckerbox. It looked like fun, but he was actually laughing at Mr Millane, wasn't he, making fun at his expense?"

Esson and Provis were both aware of how Felicity's face darkened. She did not appreciate the boy's lack of guile, not at a moment like this.

"I think that will do for now, Bart," she said. "We'll let these officers get on with other things."

She stood up to take him from the room and received no word of hindrance from the police. Youngsters are very quick to pick up if they have, without being aware, said or done the wrong thing. Bart was trembling as he left the room. Felicity Madigan was gone barely a minute, just long enough for Esson to say, "Well done, Maddie. Good teamwork. There is something here we have to probe: I don't know what it is exactly, but we have to push them until we get to the bottom of it."

"So Millane next, sir?"

He nodded grimly as Madigan came back into the room. She was nursing her anger, keeping it on the simmer.

"I'm not at all happy about the way you conducted that interview, Inspector. In my world, we don't needle young people like that, and we don't imply nasty things just to get a reaction. It is not professional."

"Our worlds are different. We will see Mr Millane now," was all he offered. When Madigan left the room again, he said quietly to Provis, "That is one impressive woman. She is doing just what she should."

"And we are doing what we have to, sir?" There was just a touch of bitter irony in her voice.

"*Ja, gewiss!*"

When Millane came into the room, Esson immediately registered the profound state of inner turmoil about which Madigan had warned him. If he was not actually incoherent, as he had been with Provis the evening before, he still looked a mess — untidy of appearance and indecisive of speech. It was about nine-thirty and

Esson accepted the offer of a mug of tea. He and Millane sat at the small square table as though they were about to conduct a job interview, or perhaps prepare a joint seminar on Chaucer. In either case, it didn't look as if Millane would contribute much. Madigan and Provis seemed to be there as mere observers, as seconds in whatever duel was about to play out.

Esson knew that he could commence as either very brisk or very gentle. The sight of the poor Englishman decided him.

"Mr Millane, I think I have the essential facts already, though I may need to come back to them. But I'll ask you what I have been asking others: what sort of a chap was this Roger," and he had to remind himself of the surname, "er... Xanthius?"

Millane shivered.

"Was. Was! How am I ever going to see his parents, or anyone, and tell them Roger was?" He gasped. "He was meant to be in my special care."

"Yes, I've heard that. And believe me, Mr Millane, I have every sympathy for your position. So far from home — and so soon to return to it. But you knew the young man best, so I must press you a little: what sort of person was he?"

Esson sat back and folded one hand over the other. He had to be calm. He did not want this man to fall to pieces, certainly not yet. Millane was, after all, the only one known to have been alone with Roger in the minutes before he died — or possibly alone with him just after he died. His benign manner had a settling effect and the distraught look and gestures abated a little.

"He was a real mixture, Inspector. He had talents — you probably know about the photography — and he could be lively and fun. He could also be arrogant. So some boys almost idolized him, and some probably didn't much trust him."

Esson drank from his mug. It was awful tea and he had only accepted it in order to create pauses. This was one of them and Millane seemed to think he had to fill it.

"A puzzle, an odd mixture, a…" but then he ran out of descriptors. He stared helplessly at Esson.

"Was he like that back in England too, or just out here?"

Millane nodded, as though that were answer enough. When he saw the raised eyebrow of the detective, he said, "Yes, both. But I suspect that he felt freer to do as he liked out here."

"And that made your keeping-a-watch role that much harder, I suppose?"

Millane nodded again but looked this time as though he were living in a scene very different from that of the motel's meeting room. Esson drank more tea then pushed the mug away. He waited, but it soon became clear that there was no response coming. Anyway, the lack of a response was eloquence itself.

"All right, Mr Millane, let's move on. Now, as I've said, I have a pretty clear idea of the timeline of yesterday's events. But I need your help on one small detail, something at the pool. You found Roger dead," (Millane flinched) "and you had to wait with him for about fifteen minutes before any help arrived. Tell me, sir: he had a daypack or something similar lying near him, didn't he?"

There was little more than a mumbled reply. "Lying on the ground, almost next to him." Millane was about to be incoherent again, Esson thought. He speeded up.

"And did you inspect, or check, that backpack?"

"No. It never occurred to me…"

"And the boy's camera, Mr Millane, where was it?"

"I don't really… I didn't see…"

"Mr Millane, it wasn't in the backpack, or anywhere else, as far as we can see. But a fanatical photographer has a camera and I sense that Roger's was never far from him — where could it have been?"

Esson leaned forward as though his own intensity could cause Millane to see what he was hitherto unaware that he had seen. All he got was a look of bewilderment.

"But you're right — we never saw him without it." Millane's eyes seemed to have opened wide. "I didn't think to hunt — I was shocked — I tried the CPR, I kept it going until I saw it was no good, there was just nothing. No, it was not near him, Inspector. I am sure of that. It was growing dark, but I am sure of that."

Esson looked across at Provis and spoke firmly.

"Sergeant, please tell Mrs Madigan that I need to see the two boys who were at the pool with Roger, together, in ten minutes."

He watched her leave the room, then faced Millane squarely again.

"Mr Millane, the boys may know something. But if you don't know, and if they don't know, then somebody else was at the pool."

Millane started violently.

"Now there was a period of maybe a quarter of an hour during which the boy was alone, injured, as we understand it, but alone at the pool. Who else could have been around? And why on earth would a stranger interfere with an injured person's camera? I can't grasp this — unless the missing camera has to do with you or one of the school party. That might make sense."

Millane's reaction this time was close to desperation. He leapt from his chair as though to loom over Esson but then sagged down more heavily and helplessly than ever.

"I am glad it's gone," he barely breathed. But before Esson could follow that up, his sergeant and Felicity Madigan came through the door. They saw Millane slumped over the table, head in hands, gasping for air. Felicity said, "I'm going to take him out now," and moved to help him up. Then she looked hard at Esson.

"You understand that I shall sit in on your next interviews. We have spoken with parents, of all the boys, I think, and they have accepted that it must be so. I can't permit a repetition of…" and she gestured at the limp figure of Millane, "or of the interview with Bart." She was not angry, Esson thought, but simply, and rightly, protective. He held his hands wide as though to say that he couldn't understand the man's collapse either.

"Yes, indeed, Mrs Madigan. That will be best. I want to be quite sure we are all on the same page here." He got up. "The sergeant and I need five minutes for a break. Then we will meet again here."

He waited until they were alone in the room, and then said to Provis, "Get on to Young — or better still, arrange more men and you go too. Search the area again and then widen out. We have to know more about this camera. And get on to Richardson. I want to know if there is any actual evidence that CPR was attempted."

She hurried away, and he hurried in search of a toilet. It truly had been awful tea.

This time, it was Esson, his mind full of loose ends, on one side of the table and three of them on the other. He had placed the chairs as he wanted them and had motioned Mrs Madigan to the one in the middle. She had nodded approvingly: she was close to both boys if they needed her. For his part, Esson had arranged it so that the two boys could not easily see each other, not without an effort. He wanted them together, so as to observe their reactions to each other as well as to his questioning, but he did not want them to be in collusion.

Arty, the tubby one, as Esson put it to himself, was quivering. Esson realised that, unless the death of Roger had occurred before the two boys went up the track to tell Millane of the fall, Arty was out of the picture. The dark one, the more intense and much sharper one, the calmer one for the moment, had never again been alone with Roger. Esson's instincts told him it was highly unlikely that they, or either one of them singly, had brought about Roger's death, but he had to proceed as though it were possible.

"Boys," he began, "I know it will be painful for you if I take you through all the events of yesterday. I won't do that," (Arty almost sobbed with relief) "but I have to ask you two important questions."

All three faces looked expectantly at him, the one in the middle severely so, the other two as though curious to discover the two crucial questions.

"So firstly, and you start us off, Shu, tell me exactly the state Roger was in when you left him at the pool."

Shu seemed reasonably collected.

"You know the big boulder?" Esson nodded. "He lay on the ground just below it, where he had fallen. Well, he fell off the boulder, but he was lying against one of those huge stepping blocks. Do you see what I mean?" Esson nodded again. "He had tried to get up but said he couldn't. He felt his head and there was blood — not heaps, not gushing, but some. We said we would go for help, because we couldn't have managed him up that path, with all those steps. Anyway, he told us to run and tell Mr Millane, didn't he, Arty? He was speaking perfectly clearly when we left him. He seemed OK."

Perhaps Shu realised that his last little comment was not very sensible. He looked away from Esson and out a window that gave onto nothing much.

"Arty — I hope I can call you that, they all seem to — can you add to that?"

"But he truly was fine, sir. He was yelling at us. We had no idea that something was — awful."

"But he wasn't fine, was he?" He sensed movement in the middle chair and quickly said, "Fair enough, you thought he was. Now, Arty, tell me plainly, why was he on the rock in the first place?"

He saw Arty try to edge back and look behind Madigan.

"No, Arty, it's your impression I want. After all, Mr Millane had instructed the three of you to pack up at once and follow him and the sick boy. It seems you didn't actually do that. So why had Roger clambered onto that boulder?"

Arty could not possibly describe what they had done, not to the policeman, even more so not with Mrs Madigan there. He was blushing furiously and said, nervously, "It was just a last photo he wanted. That's all."

It was so like Roger to want one last photo that he gazed at his teacher as though she could corroborate his evidence. She gave him a grim smile; his blushing told her that more than that had gone on.

"Yes, I see," said Esson. This was where he needed his mug of tea. He counted instead — *eins*, *zwei*, *drei* — and at *zehn,* he fixed the boys, each in turn, with a look born of much practice with tougher nuts than them.

"And so, what I need to ask you both is this: where is the camera?"

"Lying on the pebbles," said Arty at once. He had missed the force of Esson's 'is'. "He couldn't stand to get it. It flew out of his hand when he slipped" (Shu looked thoughtful — he wouldn't have put it quite like that) "and it just lay there, didn't it, Shu?"

"Well, yes, but," said the boy, but he was interrupted.

"And was it lying there when you got back with Mr Dawson, Shu? Just lying there as you left it?"

"Well, no it wasn't," said the boy with conviction. "Roger's pack was next to him. Mr Millane would have put it in there."

"Why would he do that?"

"One less thing to carry, I guess — easier if everything was in the backpack itself."

"And you saw Mr Millane put it in the backpack?"

Felicity Madigan stiffened. She did not like where this was going.

"No, but what else could have… Can't we find it?" Shu's face was now very pale; Arty just looked confused. It was all going too quickly for him.

"You see, boys, and Mrs Madigan," and Esson sat more comfortably now, the hands calmly folded again, "Mr Millane never saw it again. And you never saw it again. And Roger couldn't move. And if," — he let a beat pass — "you are telling me the truth, the inescapable conclusion is that someone else was there. And I have to ask myself, who could that have been?"

He could see the burden his avalanche of Ands placed on them. He waited. Then he went back over the events of the fall once more and let them go. He wanted another look at the pool itself, so declined any more of the motel's dubious refreshments. As he drove away, Felicity Madigan beckoned to the boys, ushered them back into the room and sat them down.

"Come on, boys, you know why I want to talk some more. There was more going on at the pool than you have told us. We've been so shocked by Roger's death that we haven't asked you much, but now I have to. Come on — tell me why you took so long."

She paused. She wanted to ask about the camera but decided to wait, to see first whether the boys would be straight with her. At first Shu just shrugged his shoulders, but then he gave a helpless laugh.

"You and your blushing, Arty."

Arty looked furiously at him, not because they would have to tell the truth — that was inevitable, he saw that — but because, through all his years at the college, he had been mocked as 'the blushing boy'. He couldn't help it, and to be sneered at by his friend Shu was more than he could take. He was about to retort angrily at Shu when Mrs Madigan carried on.

"There must have been something to blush about. I'm getting impatient. We have to be honest about what happened. It's the only way. It doesn't mean you're in trouble, but it has to be."

Shu shrugged again, but this time it was in submission. "It hasn't got anything to do with Roger dying."

"But it's part of the whole picture, isn't it? Come on now." She felt certain that she was about to hear the story of the missing minutes at the pool. "If I'm to deal properly with this, I have to know."

Arty glared at Shu. He knew Shu had greater powers of resistance.

"You see, Roger had been taking silly photos of us — standing on that stupid dog, pretending to fall off a cliff, that kind of thing. And he had been at us and at us for one of the two of us," and Arty gulped, aware that Shu was staring out the window again, apparently remote from what was being said, "well, with no clothes on. In the open, you know. And when Mr Millane had to head off with Bart, he... we... he took us, by the side of the pool. It was just in fun, a dare," he finished lamely.

"I see." She was steely. "Shu?" All she got was the briefest of nods. "And had he ever taken such photographs before? Anytime?"

"He tried once in the shower room, didn't he, Shu?"

Shu came back to them. He seemed to be in great pain but the misery, or confusion, or whatever it was, was directed almost entirely, brutally, at himself. And perhaps at Mr Millane, too.

"Oh yes, he tried, but we told him to bugger off." He looked almost wildly at his teacher and screamed at her, "Why did I let him? Why did I ever co-operate with such a creep? He was fun; he would challenge..."

To Arty's horror, his friend broke down in huge sobs, not of grief, but rather of despair born out of an overwhelming awareness of his parents, who were sacrificing so much.

"True enough, Shu — but at what cost? To all of you — and now to him?"

They both stared at her: what weird connection was she making? They hated and feared what they had done for Roger, but after all, he had fallen off a rock — that was all. For Felicity Madigan, it was not all.

"Now listen to me. Is it possible, did Roger ever threaten in any way to use any of the pictures he took against you or against anyone else? Come on, Shu — you called him a creep. Did he threaten you?"

She had barked out those last words much more fiercely than she had intended, a mark of her own escalating anxiety.

"He wouldn't have dared," grunted Shu.

"But he did," cried Arty. "He stood on that rock and said he could make trouble for us, and for Millane, that Parslow would..."

He shuddered to a halt. Shu now had his head in his hands. He was seeing nothing, nothing except a school career now in ruins, of parents shamed, of prospects blighted, all because he had allowed himself to find an element of fun in an arrogant person who wasn't even one of them, one who had ultimately returned the adulation by treachery, betrayal. Shu had always thought he was in full control of the situation and could call a halt whenever he wished; now he could not bear to acknowledge how he had been controlled throughout. Mrs Madigan was speaking to him.

"Shu, be honest with me. Did others, did most of the student group, know that Roger was acting like this, that he might use the photos against you?"

"They didn't much like him." He was trying very hard to focus on her question. "But they never said… no, I don't think they saw that side of him. And I never believed he would." He sighed, then said, as though for once he couldn't keep up with her, "But why does it matter anyway?"

She did not immediately answer and the boys looked at her intently. They were typical in this: that, though they loved to pretend that teachers, even senior ones, could be kept conveniently in the dark, they nevertheless looked to those same teachers to lighten that darkness when they could not do so themselves.

"It matters," she said, and it took a huge effort to prevent her voice from shaking, "because if you are the only ones who knew that Roger was threatening to use the camera against you, and if that camera is missing, it might look as though you are the ones who made it disappear." She paused, and then decided to risk it. "And if you've not 'fessed up about this," (they boggled at her unnatural colloquialism) "then what else have you not told us?"

For once, Arty's colour was dead white.

"You can't think… Oh, Mrs Madigan, you can't think that we had anything to do with his fall. You can't think that?" He barely breathed it out. "He just fell."

"Yes, Arty. Yes, Shu — I believe you. But there must be nothing except the complete truth from now on. Now," and she resorted to acting deputy briskness again, "I urgently suggest you do not talk to the others about our conversation, or the latest interview with Inspector Esson. They will gossip about it and that will only obscure the truth. For myself, I must think - and you must need some morning tea."

She looked at her watch — it was just after eleven. "Off you go then."

They moved to the door. Shu could not face her but Arty turned and said, "You must believe us." She gave him a small, reassuring smile, knowing it would do no good. She had planted the seed and she couldn't unplant it now. But she did not need time alone to think; instead, she went immediately in search of Dennis Millane.

X

Sergeant Provis had been able to assemble a team of five, including one regarded as the sharpest eyes in the area, and by mid-morning on Wednesday the fifth they were gathered at the Pool of Siloam. It was still very grey — not actually raining, but the air seemed so clingingly damp that it might as well have been. Provis got them to start on the pool area and then radiate out, ignoring, for the moment, the path by which they had come down.

The stream was flowing, not rapidly but steadily, and all the rocks were dangerously slippery. She noticed that the guys straight from the police station in Katoomba had much better boots for clambering than herself, so she took the path leading in the direction of Gladstone Road, got two to comb the nearby ferns and bush and sent two more down the stream. Within five minutes, there was a shout. Provis ran back, edged behind the great boulder from which Roger had fallen and looked down the tumbling watercourse.

"Camera, Sergeant! Just as you thought," came from Constable Young.

"Well done — but don't touch! How badly smashed is it?"

She beckoned Sharp-eyes over, told him to get a large evidence bag and sent him down.

"It's wedged between two rocks. Otherwise, it would be fully under water. The lens is down — I've no idea about damage."

She would have to be content with that.

"Nothing else with it? No camera case or anything? No sign of the innards ripped out?"

But all her questions received only a 'can't tell anything' gesture and she had to wait until the camera was retrieved and brought back to her. She lay it down on a clear plastic sheet. Like all of them, she was wearing gloves.

"So what has happened here, guys? Reconstruct for me."

Even Aaron Young was only sketchily familiar with the events and personalities of the day before. He remained silent. But Constable Sharples — 'Sharp-eyes' — was useful.

"Well, we saw it wedged there, as Aaron said. It could only have got into that position if thrown from above, very likely from up here," and he pointed to the boulder. "Right?"

Young was just about to give his assent when Maddie came in with, "Or placed there?" They could only nod that it could be so.

"But why, then," she followed up, "would anyone place it there? It's not as though it was being hidden for later retrieval. Look at it!"

The smashed lens and dented casing were evidence enough. It had clearly been thrown and that prompted Provis to say, with some degree of eagerness, that the same question — why on earth would one do it? — applied if it was thrown from where they all were.

"Look, if you wanted to get rid of it, then you'd hide it, bury it maybe. Or you'd take it away to another location, where no one would ever look. You wouldn't toss it carelessly no more than twenty metres away and not even check to see that it was concealed. It doesn't make sense."

"Unless," said Young, "you only wanted to know that it was wrecked."

"Yes, I can see that. But even then," and she fell into thought. Did whoever threw it, check even so much as that? There was still so much they did not know, and too much guessing was not helpful. "*Nicht so gut,*" she caught herself muttering.

They were packing their gear when she suddenly turned to Young.

"Aaron, you and Sharples stay on a bit. We'll leave one car for you. I had only just started on the other path out," she gestured to it as she handed him some keys, "and I'd hate to have missed something. Just follow it through and see if there's anything that suggests even a trace of others being around. It's a long shot, but give it a try."

She and the other two men started the climb out to Gordon Falls reserve, bearing the precious, enigmatic camera. She was pleased to have something to report to Esson but she had little idea what it signified. They knew that the camera had been lying on the sand; now they could be pretty sure it had been pitched down the creek from up on the boulder. That was where Roger had taken photographs, so they were told. How did it all connect up? Maybe Esson would put it all together — but he would probably try to explain it to her in German.

XI

"I've talked about it enough, Felicity. I can't manage it again."

"I'm sorry, Dennis," she said as she led him into the meeting room, wishing it wasn't so four-square and clinical. "It's not so much about yesterday as about some other things about Roger. I don't want any of us to be under suspicion — and that means I don't want any of us to be concealing things from the police. You have to help me here."

"What about Roger, then? None of us really trusted him, and I was really looking forward to parting ways. But his odd habits didn't lead to… this!"

He was becoming very agitated again and his last, arms-flung-wide gesture seemed to include the sterile meeting room, Roger's challenging temperament, the whole disaster.

"It's those odd habits I need to ask you about. Now, I have learned from Shu and Arty that, when you and Bart left them at the pool yesterday, supposedly packing up, our two boys stripped naked and Roger, from on top of that boulder, photographed them. Not only that, but he suggested — I'm not quite sure if he threatened —

that he would use the compromising photo to embarrass, or worse, his two friends and even yourself. You must tell me if he said anything to you, at any time, that would gel with such a threat."

Before the last sentence had begun, however, Millane had gone pale and was trembling.

"What?" he whispered. "Did he say that he wanted to make me look incompetent, or unprofessional? Did he say something like that?"

"I think he might have. He would tell Allan Parslow, or…"

But she had no clear idea what Roger might have said. And it wasn't the point.

"Dennis, had there been other evidence of this side of him? Tell me."

Millane was still trembling, though perhaps it was in recognition of his own narrow escape.

"Once, last year, his final year at the Hangar, he became aware of another boy, another senior, having clandestine meetings with a girl. He apparently told the other boy he had photographic evidence. If he did, we never saw it. Then the year finished. I wasn't close to the matter, and I knew nothing more of the incident. But it did warn me that I had to be careful around him."

Felicity's mind flitted to Parslow and how furious he would be that another school had foisted on him this untrustworthy loose cannon of a kid. She said to Millane, "Was there ever a hint of blackmail, even in a small, joking way? I haven't asked Shu and Arty that, not directly. But I'll have to — and Esson will have to know about all this."

She waited, and waited again. Eventually he spoke, low and miserably.

"Just a whisper. A comment or two I overheard at the valedictory dinner in June, shortly before I came here. A hint? — barely even that. But I think his peers suspected something. I passed it on to the Head but it was all so vague, and then the year ended, I was packing to come to your school, he said to let it go — and I did. It was easiest, wasn't it?"

It had poured from him, a waterfall of words.

"Easiest for whom? Yes, it probably was. And I would guess, most dangerous, too."

"Dangerous, Felicity? But nothing has come of it. The lad fell and hit his head. No one has tried to… to… to silence him."

Felicity thought about that.

"No, I suppose not. But we have to tell the police what we know. They are already suspicious about the absence of the camera. And when I do tell them, I can't control what conclusions they might jump to."

At her words, Millane sank back in his chair and covered his face in his hands. He had been so close to going home; now it seemed that there would be no end to the misery, the terror. So close — but was he never to escape from the entanglements of oh-so-clever Roger Xanthius?

XII

He needed to see the pool once more, but on leaving the motel, he discovered that the need for a proper drink and a moment's quiet contemplation was even greater. He drove back into Leura, which was unusually empty for a school holiday — put it down to the grim weather! — and found a park just off the pathway to Lily's Pad. He was known there, and armed with an excellent strong flat white and a huge Anzac biscuit, he found a quietish corner. Despite those luxuries, he was not comfortable.

He did not like the missing periods of time — say five to ten minutes after Millane and the vomiting boy left the pool, too much time for just a quick pack-up; then fifteen minutes after Roger fell, if he did fall, while the two boys found help; then another fifteen minutes or so when Millane was alone with… a corpse? Or had Millane not tried CPR after all? Had he turned the still living Roger into a corpse? Did that explain the two wounds to the back of Roger's head? Somewhere in all that a camera had disappeared. Meanwhile, a young man with a busted ankle and a supposedly slight bump on the head had died, possibly of another blow to the head. But then, Richardson had seemed ambivalent about the two blows. Another thing — could he believe Shu and Arty? They had had plenty of time to agree on a narrative if Roger had already been dead, and they were obviously concealing something. He finished the coffee, got up, waved at Lily (he always called her that, hadn't even bothered to ask her real name) and went off still munching the Anzac. It was excellent — syrupy and crisp and chewy, all at once. He wished he could put the diverse elements of this case together so neatly.

He arrived at Gordon Falls reserve just as Maddie Provis and colleagues were getting into a car. She beckoned him across and beamed.

"This'll be the camera, sir. Maybe twenty metres downstream, wedged between rocks. We don't know how damaged it is."

His response was all she had expected.

"*Wunderbar*! *Sehr gut, Fraulein*. Sorry, Sergeant — but this is just what I was hoping for. Get it up to Katoomba pronto and wait there until you can get a line on what might be possible. Let's meet at the motel at... say... three. I'm going to have another look at the pool myself."

"Fine, sir. You might see Aaron Young — I sent him and Sharples — yes, sir, that's his real name — to have a look down the path that leads the other way, to Gladstone Road, just in case."

"I've no idea what that might reveal," he said. "Which is the best of reasons for doing it. There is such a lot we don't know — yet. Go have some lunch, and

I'll see you at three. *Nicht vergessen!*" He shook an admonitory finger at her in his glee. Just then it began to pour.

He knelt in the teeming rain at the stepping stones below the boulder, then went round the boulder and looked down the stream. He looked back up — he could see bits of the track, the falls themselves, the other path that went off to Lyrebird, on which there seemed to be some kind of viewpoint, a vantage point overlooking the pool. Any traces of movement would be gone now. Even as he had come down the steep path, parts of it were boggy, others swampy, some already miniature lakes. It was pretty pointless — he need not have come down in this wretched rain. Just then, Constables Young and Sharples came from the other path into the clearing. They too had only regular uniforms on and looked very miserable.

"Well, friends," said Esson. "Here's a fine place for a meeting."

Young scowled at him; the other constable, even more unused to Esson, did not know what to think.

"Find anything, then?"

"We went through to the other end. Most of it was slush, especially on the way back. We picked up just a couple of chocolate wrappers — the sergeant said you never can tell — and this piece of paper. Not a thing otherwise. No footprints left, or…"

"No, of course not." Esson interrupted the young man and reached for the stray bit of paper. It was a lined A4 sheet, maybe from a pad, with writing mostly washed into indecipherability. He gazed at it and handed it back.

"Get it up to Katoomba, guys. You might see Sergeant Provis there — if so, tell her about it. Well done — I think."

He sent them on their way and took a last look around the desolate pool. It told him nothing — but that might be important in itself. After all, some of the human participants in this business were not telling him all they knew either. Why should the pool be any different? The rain fell more heavily than ever. He shrugged and began the ascent. The path was getting slushier by the minute. He stumbled and one knee went into a mud puddle. He cursed, though not in German this time. Home — shower — change — lunch: he had plenty of time before three.

XIII

Of course he did, heaps of time, so he sent Provis a message telling her he would be at the station at two thirty. She too had gone to change, but they needed to bring each other up to date, to make sure they were missing nothing, before the next meeting at the motel.

"Any forensic news then, Sergeant? The camera?"

"Nothing from it yet, sir. And they won't even say that there will be — the smashing and the rain, you know. But it is Roger's: I went by the motel, to ask that question and that only. No doubt about it, they said."

"Who said?" His tone was somewhat sharp. "And they know that we have it, then?" He seemed, to Provis, unreasonably agitated. "Can't be helped," he muttered.

Provis was taken aback.

"Sorry, sir. I didn't want us to spend time on a false lead. Is there…?"

"Not to worry. I was just thinking that we might have kept them in suspense a bit longer. That sometimes… but never mind, it might even work in our favour. Who can tell? Also…" and it took her a moment to register it as a German connective, "it could have been thrown there by Millane, Shu or Arty, and I think we might be about to find out why, or could it have been by someone else, in the brief time Roger was alone? If it's that, then we are really in the dark, with no idea at all of who — or why."

He scratched his chin; Provis was sensible enough just to wait for whatever was to follow.

"Anything about those papers?"

"No. I'm assuming just chance rubbish."

"Yes. Probably. I was hoping... Well, let's go back to the motel."

They scurried through the rain to Esson's car, and before he drove off, he said to her, "You know, this school we're dealing with is a strange animal. No request for them to go anywhere, do anything else, and plenty of shock, but not the remotest sign of grief." He shrugged his shoulders, as though it were impossible to penetrate to the inner thoughts of those whose position in and whose view of the world must be so very different from his own.

"Remind me," he said between clenched teeth, "to ask only for water. Now let's go and confront Mrs Madigan again."

Perhaps it was she who confronted them. She must have been keeping watch, because she met them in the carpark of the motel, just as yet another shower of rain began to blow through.

"Come in quickly, out of this miserable weather. And yes," in response to Esson's eyebrows, "I was waiting for you. I want to speak to you before you do anything more."

She ushered them into the meeting room. It felt very chill and Provis went at once to a wall heater that began to blow out vile smelling warm air. But Felicity Madigan was all business. They sat.

"You need to know," she said without any preliminaries, "that Roger might have been a very fine photographer — but he was also one who used, or at least threatened to use, his photos to embarrass or to compromise others. There is a sketchy account of one such incident back in England, and yesterday, just before he fell, he took a photo of undressed Shu and Arty," (it was so hard for her!) "And made at least a joking comment that he could use it against them. But," and here she was insistent, "those boys, and Dennis Millane, all insist that they have no idea how the camera went missing. I believe them on that point. There," and she breathed a sigh, "I had to make this plain to you."

She sat back a little, knowing that she had omitted one aspect of what Roger might have threatened. Esson's hand began automatically to feel around for a mug that wasn't there.

"You know," he said eventually, "that we have found the camera. I take it that it will contain that compromising photo, if not more."

Madigan simply nodded. Now that she had told them, it didn't seem to make much difference whether the photo was actually recoverable or not. On the whole better not — if only for the sake of Shu and Arty.

"Mrs Madigan, I had half-suspected something like this and the camera will confirm it. Now, you have presented it all as something rather jocular…"

(Had she? she thought: it didn't feel like that.)

"…but it may have been much more serious. It sounds like a matter of blackmail to me."

He let the ugly word sit there.

"It's not a nice thought, is it?" he pursued relentlessly. "And yet it would explain, in the most obvious way, why a person might want to destroy the evidence — and perhaps also destroy the perpetrator. You can't expect me not to consider that."

She was white but determined not to be overwhelmed.

"It is your job to consider it. Mine is a very different job and I do not believe for one moment…"

But she could not carry that sentence to its all too logical conclusion. She could not bring herself to consider that one of her boys… No, she could not go there. Instead, she made a kind of retreat.

"We are not hiding anything from you, Inspector. That's precisely why I intercepted you, to tell you what I did. I also need to tell you that Dennis Millane is still in a state of very severe shock. I beg you to leave him, for today, please."

Esson thought that if the request were made purely out of compassion he would agree to it, but not if it were made in order to shield. He said, "I don't see why Millane, or the boys, would dispose of the camera in such a fashion — not really disposing of it at all, was it?"

Felicity breathed more easily.

"Unless, of course, they heard, or thought they heard, someone else about and had to act in haste."

He waited for her to gasp, but she held up. He had an inspiration.

"We don't know whether anyone else was there, but there was that other group of teenagers nearby. Now, if they..."

"But I don't understand." She tried to be analytical. "We left them deep in their studies. I don't see how they come into it."

"Neither do I. But I will know, soon enough. Mrs Madigan, there are too many unexplained matters for me to say to you that it was an unfortunate accident and leave it at that. And if you are right, and your people know nothing of the camera, then someone else *was* there. So I must continue to investigate, to probe. I will need to..."

Exactly what he might need was never said. There was a knock and the door opened, revealing Guy Somerville.

"Are you still at it, then?" he said to his colleague.

"Come in, Guy," she said, clearly quite happy at the interruption. She turned back to Esson. "I had asked Guy to give me fifteen minutes and then to come in. I have told you what I needed to — but now we have something else to talk about. After all…"

"I wondered how long it would be until this. Do sit with us, Mr Somerville. You want to talk about continuing with your school excursion."

Of the two teachers, only Somerville was at all taken aback. Felicity was practical.

"But of course, we do. That's what we're here for, and whatever your views on the death of Roger, it is quite definite that nearly all of us had no part in it. For myself, I am convinced that it was all. I see no reason why we should not undertake our planned activities tomorrow. We raise it with you just as a courtesy really."

She felt rather as though she had played all her cards at once. Esson was impressed: she was bold, and she was no fool. For the first time in the whole interview, he looked across at Maddie Provis. But that was only in lieu of a mug of tea.

"I understand your position. I want your guarantee that you will all return here tomorrow evening. And I need to know your planned date of departure — I can't guarantee not to insist that you change it. Do you expect Mr Millane to go out with you, if you go?"

She stared at him. She could be just as blunt.

'As to the first, yes. The second — Saturday. The third — we may not know until the morning. Satisfied?"

He was. Very. He said, "For the moment, I leave it to you how much, or how little, of all this you communicate to your staff and your students. I imagine I will want to see you tomorrow night, or Friday morning. Sergeant Provis and I have a number of other things to check in the interim." Then he thought that the edginess of the last few minutes ought to be put aside. "And I do thank you, I mean it, for being so forthright. That can only help — all of us."

She did not smile, just barely nodded. She wanted, needed to believe Shu and Arty. But she was no longer quite so sure about Dennis Millane.

"Let's get the group together, Guy, and tell them about tomorrow.

It was as though the two police officers had ceased to exist. Esson was used to that. Once again it was a matter of control. People needed to manage a life to which police probing posed a very real threat. When they sat again in his car, which immediately started to fog up, he said to his sergeant, "We have to find out about that group of teenagers — I hope they are on to it back at the station. And we have to get inside the camera. Let's make a start now. I think tomorrow will answer some of our questions. "

Provis nodded. "*Sehr gut*," she said under her breath, but not so far under as to avoid a glare from Esson, and then a very comradely smile.

XIV

They arrived back at the police station in the late afternoon, ready to begin some detailed searching. Esson was highly excited, feeling that he was about to see clearly the pattern that had so far eluded him. One or two pieces of information, something tangible, was what he was after. He got more than he had bargained for.

Provis's desk — Esson hadn't bothered to organise one for himself yet — was awash with sticky yellow notelets. He was delighted; to Provis it seemed like too much detail. Aaron Young, who was to go off duty at five, was waiting enthusiastically, ready to fill them in. He was not pleased to be told to find some strong coffee first.

Sergeant Anson Shah came across from a small space, a cubby-hole, if you like, on one side of the main workroom. Maddie Provis smiled warmly at him.

"You're looking well, Anson. Making it through the day, OK?"

The man frowned at her, but it was not an unfriendly frown. He had returned to work only on Tuesday, after an unexpectedly severe bout of the 'flu, amounting almost to pneumonia, and the medical advice had been to keep him inside for the rest of the week. It turned out to have been good advice: Shah had taken all the scraps of information so far collected and had organised them effectively, had followed up with forensics, had taken phone calls — and had loved every minute of it.

"I'm fine, thank you," he said with just a touch of testy impatience. "I'm ready to give you a briefing on all this," gesturing at Provis's desk, "as soon as you like. You'll find Young very useful too."

Constable Young returned just then with coffee and gave Shah a grateful look. He knew how easy it was for a mere constable to be sidelined. Esson, coffee in hand, was already looking over the collection of sticky notes.

"Let me give you a quick overview, sir. The folder on the left contains photos. Some will not surprise you, others may."

Esson grinned at that. He would evince no surprise.

"Anything about the scrap of paper?"

"No, sir. It's in the folder with the photos but it was pretty badly water damaged. Some figures maybe — hard to tell even that."

"I thought there might be. It fits."

Maddie thought she could follow him; the others plainly couldn't.

"Then," continued Shah, "there's information about your three teenagers. Aaron, do you want to explain? You did some of the phoning."

Barely able to contain his excitement, the young man began.

"There are not that many high schools to check, you see, but they are all on holidays."

Esson's look told him to cut straight to the outcome. He tried to stay calm, not let his agitated breathing spoil his words.

"So, the boy is Alex, his address is there. His principal has probably alerted him, or his family, so they'll expect a visit. We have the names and addresses of the other two, the girls, also. The principal obviously hoped we wouldn't start with them."

"And why would that have been?"

Young was good on information, but such a question took him too far into the realm of speculation. He merely shrugged his shoulders. Shah came to the rescue.

"I think he assumed that Alex — er, Jamieson — would have been the organiser."

Esson looked doubtful. Was the principal offering them good information or simply putting the view that suited his own purposes? Esson harboured severe doubts about school principals. However, he had the lead he had longed for.

"We'll be at his house at seven," he said to Maddie. He scanned the sheet of names: it was a north side of the highway address, not five minutes away. "And I'll take this paper with me. Make a copy, please, to keep here."

Nods all around, but again only Provis's showed signs of comprehension.

"Now, these yellow notes?"

"This is interesting, and unexpected, sir," Shah continued. "News of the incident — a death in the mountains always makes the Sydney news — has caused a Mrs Rose Shillingworth to get in touch. She and her husband want you to meet them in the morning, the 9.06 train."

"And what part have they to play?" asked Esson acerbically. He had never heard of them. It sounded like an unnecessary distraction.

"They've rung twice, sir, to make sure of the time. Aaron?" He was determined to give the young man every opportunity.

"They were in the area, sir." He pointed to one of the notelets. "They are part of a group called the Western Sydney Walkers and they were in the Pool of Siloam area yesterday afternoon." He seemed to hesitate. "They thought you would want to see them."

Young was no longer quite as sure of himself as he had been. He waited. Esson was in one of his thinking out aloud states.

"It's too much to hope for. What if they could narrow down the timing, make it clear to us exactly when he died? It's a long shot." He came out of it. "Thank you, Constable. And you, too, Sergeant. This is all most efficient and helpful. Maddie, we'll look through this folder, and then we'll see the Jamiesons at seven. They don't know when we are coming?" He checked again with Shah.

"Not to the exact time, sir. We imagine that they have been forewarned."

He nodded, and then he and Maddie drew two chairs to the desk. He gave her a look which said, *I think we know what we'll find here*, and opened the folder of photographs.

They must have been arranged in chronological order, the oldest ones on top, because the first couple meant nothing at all. Esson flipped to the back and started to work in the opposite direction. He found he could follow the day easily enough. Roger had taken a very complete record. The last photos were of Arty and Shu naked by the pool — three photos, more or less identical, the boys looking up at the camera, not at each other, though perhaps Shu's smile became more frozen through the sequence. Well, it had been a cold afternoon to be without their clothes. There were photos of the whole group at Siloam and some looking in every direction from it, and a couple looking down on it from a point higher up. That must have been the vantage point Esson had noted earlier. He should check it out, perhaps. Then there were photos at Lyrebird Dell. There were interesting general photos, but also of the three who were not part of the college group and of a recess, a semi-cave. The three were looking away from the camera but Esson added one of those snaps — Roger, as always, had taken several — to his pile for that evening. Then there were photos of Katoomba Street — nothing of note there — and of other moments earlier in the week. Then there were the two photos which dated from before Roger even came to Australia. He paused.

"I'm going to get a hamburger and look at all this more closely. Then we've got at least one more interview for tonight. Coming?"

She didn't want a hamburger. He saw her face and laughed.

"At least come and help me with the photos — make sure I don't miss anything."

"Now that will be a pleasure," she said.

While Esson and Provis, who stuck to the coleslaw, ate and examined the photographs, it happened that Felicity Madigan was missing out on the motel dinner. Allan Parslow had rung. She took her mobile back to her own room and listened to the familiar voice. He was not happy.

"So, then, I have gathered that the Xanthius family is quite chaotic. The Head of Chaddlehangar can't actually disparage them, though I would have done so gleefully in a case like this, but it seems as though the father is in Switzerland and hasn't been seen for some time. There's plenty of money but not much common sense, and maybe not even much real concern for Roger. But we think Mrs X is coming out on the first available flight — unless, perhaps, it interferes with a vital drinks' engagement."

"I still expect to drive back on Saturday, Allan. There is no justification for keeping us here. I suppose there could be some doubt about Dennis, and about Shu, possibly Arty. You've been in touch with their parents, I presume."

"Of course, I have, several times. And with the other parents too. I just tell them that you are dealing with it all and to remain calm." His impatience with it all flared again. "Just make sure they're all with you on Saturday."

It might not be her decision, of course, thought Felicity. For a second or two, she tried to imagine Parslow and Esson face to face, each determined to wrest control of the situation from the other. It would be a feisty battle! Then she clicked back into reality.

"And Mrs Millane?" she said.

"Dreadfully anxious. Wants to be there with him — but then there is the child."

Odd for a school man to be irritated by the presence of a child, she thought. But she knew Parslow well enough — easily irritated by anything that got in the way of his plans. He had to be the one pulling all the strings.

"I take it we have your encouragement to complete as much of the fieldwork as we can. I need to keep the boys — all of us — occupied. In some ways I'd rather come home, but I don't think the authorities are ready for that, not yet."

"You mean this man Esson, don't you? Don't let him control you, Felicity."

She didn't answer at once and he said, "I'm sorry. You're in an awful position. I assume Guy is a real support."

"As always," she said, nodding vigorously even though he couldn't see it. "We'll proceed with our plans and try to make the boys feel that it is all as normal as possible. But I can't really pretend that it is, especially not for Shu and Arty. They are feeling too many things at once."

Parslow had no solution for her. "I'll keep you informed of anything at this end. The Brillias want to see me tomorrow. I really have very little I can tell them."

"They may have something to tell you, though."

She was not quite sure why she had put it that way.

"Oh, really? Now I'm interested. Take care, Felicity — all of you."

He could be an exciting Head, full of plans, always ready for change, sometimes even ready to turn things topsy-turvy, but ordinary, everyday warmth was not his strong point. Felicity went to see if any of the roast chicken was left — it had smelled good!

XV

The house was a pleasant mountains timber bungalow, tucked away in a small street on the north side, only a minute or two from the hospital. Once, residents of that street would have felt that the town was just a few steps away, but the highway and the railway line together served to cut them off. It certainly made their side-street a quiet place at seven o'clock on a drizzly winter's evening.

Esson and Provis, as they walked up the short path, surveyed the broad veranda and the half circle of leadlight above the front door. It was a solid and comfortable house. It suited the Jamiesons very well: he had a senior administrative position at the hospital and she was a teacher at one of the local primary schools. Alex, in his last year at school, was their only child.

It was Mrs Jamieson who turned on the veranda light and opened the door. The most inviting smells of curry wafted out. Esson held up his ID and explained that they had come to see Alex.

"The school rang, the principal," said Mrs Jamieson. "This is not the best time."

"There is almost never a good time. But we do need to see your son — with you and your husband there too, of course." She opened the screen door and he added, "We think Alex can help us fill in the picture of an incident out in the bush."

"You see, my husband is not in yet. I feel he should be here." She was nervous and intense in a fluttery sort of way. "Of course, we have seen the news and I've already asked Alex about it. I don't think he can tell you much."

There was no help for it. She led them down the central hallway as she spoke, to a living room at the rear that looked out, through a wall of windows, to a back yard that ran down to a deep gully. All of that would have been visible on a summer's evening. On this miserable day, heavy curtains had been pulled across. The room was very warm — a slow combustion stove was working almost too well.

Alex was standing beside a large TV screen, waiting for them. Esson saw in him a confident, maybe assertive young man, used to getting his own way. He told himself not to make hasty judgements. Maddie Provis was smiling at the boy, too ready, Esson thought, to take him at his own valuation.

"It's good of you to see us," he began. "Important, too. We hope that you can help us with our jigsaw — who was where and when, that sort of thing."

Mrs Jamieson gestured them to seats. "We can't add a lot," she said, looking at Alex rather than at Esson.

"But we'll try." If she had intended to be positive and optimistic, she had failed. Esson couldn't see why she would have anything to offer them at all.

"No, I don't imagine you can, Mrs Jamieson. But Alex and his friends might be able to. We'll want to speak to them too, of course. Each person always notices different things."

Alex spoke for the first time. He was blunt, perhaps a little too blunt.

"What do you want to talk about? The group of people, where somebody has died?"

"Of course." The boy was obviously trying to get it over with as quickly as possible. "Now, Alex, one thing we're trying to do is get a clear timeline. So begin by telling us when you first saw them."

The lad desperately wanted to say, "What makes you think I saw them at all?" He had told his mother some things, not by any means everything. For example, he had not told her of his annoyance at the camera boy.

"It was some time in the afternoon. I wasn't looking at a watch."

Esson was about to get grumpy. Provis jumped in.

"That'd be right, Alex. Where did they come from? Just give us a picture. You three, for example, you were at Lyrebird."

He was startled, which showed. He made a quick decision, which also showed.

"The three of us went out on Monday morning. We planned a two-day study break. More study than break, if we could manage it. We were nearly finished, almost ready to pack up, by the middle of the afternoon yesterday when this other mob came lumbering in. They asked us how far to the Pool of Siloam and we pointed them to the path. They didn't have far to go."

Alex managed a tight smile and looked at his mother. Esson wondered if that, and no more, was their agreed statement. He naturally wanted more.

"They stayed in your area for... how long?"

"A few minutes only. One of their teachers or leaders took them to one side of the clearing, waiting for the stragglers. Then they moved on."

It was Maddie's turn again. A tag-team approach often led somewhere; at the least, it kept the interviewee guessing as to where the next question was coming from.

"Tell us about the young man with the camera. What was he doing?"

"I think he took some photos. I didn't pay much attention to him."

"Oh really?" said Esson. "We have the impression that he was a rather in-your-face person."

Alex just shrugged and his mother, scrambling to keep up, tried to intervene. "Of course, Alex couldn't form any impression of someone they had just..."

"We know he took photos, though," Esson went on. "Including of your group."

As though on cue, Maddie handed him the folder. He had put Roger's record of the stop at Lyrebird on top of the pile. He spoke now as though simply recapitulating what they all knew.

"You can see he took general views of the clearing, but very particularly of you three, of your study area, of the beer cans and so on, and of your cave-like shelter, the sleeping bags. He was quite thorough, this young man."

"If you say so." Alex was becoming agitated, though not in his mother's fluttery way. There was some conflict going on in him and they could not tell whether it was because he knew more than he wanted to say or simply because Mother was not meant to know about the beer cans. And if he had not told her that, what else hadn't he wanted to mention? It was surely more than the beer cans. It had, Esson surmised, something to do with Roger. But the boy turned to defensive mode. "I didn't want anything to do with him. I went back into the shelter and they moved on."

"To the pool?"

"Well, they went that way."

As though to emphasise her next question, Maddie held out a hand towards him from where she sat on the sofa.

"And did you see them again? Or see Roger again?"

He was a quick-minded young man.

"No, we never saw that group again. They did not come back past us."

When one is leaving bits out, it is comforting to know which bits it is safe, and important, to leave in.

Alex and his mother seemed to feel that that ended the matter; she even began to get up.

"But Roger, the young man with the camera, did you see him again?"

Alex still felt comfortable.

"No, he never came back our way."

"Well, we know that, Alex," said Maddie. "He died at the pool."

The simplicity of her statement was shocking, brutal. Mrs Jamieson wanted to clarify matters.

"It is awful, yes, but if he never came back that way, then…"

"Then that's all you can tell us, is it, Alex?"

The boy nodded firmly at Esson — that was all. "OK then." Esson followed another line. "We also need to know if any other groups or individuals came through, yesterday, at any time. Did you see anyone else?"

This was safe ground.

"Earlier, soon after we'd had lunch, a group of maybe six or eight oldies — sorry, Mum. They walked straight through, barely stopped. I think the three of us were tidying up in the cave."

"And nobody else?"

"I know it's school holidays, but no, yesterday was really quiet in our area."

Maddie started to neaten the pile of photos, an action that seemed to signal an end to the interview.

"Just one more thing," she said, keeping her hand on the file. "Just so we are clear. When did you three leave, and by what route?"

For the first time, Alex started to mumble.

"Er, I think… er… about half an hour after them. We finished off our study and packed up."

"And back to Gordon Falls reserve. Bertie was going to bring the car there, wasn't he?" Mrs Jamieson had plainly rehearsed this point earlier too.

"Well, yes, we…"

There was the sound of a key in the front door, of a bag being put down and an overcoat being taken off. Mother and son looked up the hallway. Were they glad he had come, just at that point? A tall man, very tall actually, came wearily into the room and stopped short. They had all risen.

"Elaine? Alex? What is going on here?"

Esson had already produced his ID. "Police, Mr Jamieson. You probably know of the sad death of a young Englishman out in the bush yesterday. We need to interview all those who were anywhere in the vicinity." He paused as Mr Jamieson went to stand with his wife and son. "It was a tragic happening. Alex and his two friends were amongst those who came across that school group during the day."

"So I understand." Mr Jamieson turned briskly to Esson. Just the remains of his Scottish ancestry were evident in his voice. "And have you heard what you wanted to hear?"

"Wanted, Mr Jamieson? All we want is to build up a clear picture of the events of the day."

"And Alex has helped you do that? Excellent. I must say the curry smells good." He beamed at his wife, then looked back at Esson. His meaning was unmistakable: "Off you go and leave us to our family dinner." Mrs Jamieson joined in.

"The curry has been waiting a while, dear."

He put an arm affectionately around her. Esson turned to Alex.

"So Bertie arrived with your car, then, at Gordon Falls reserve? How did that arise? Where had the car been?"

"That was the arrangement," was all Alex managed.

"And this Bertie, I wonder if he saw anything," said Maddie with an innocent smile. She opened a pad. "His name and address, Alex?"

Alex gulped. His father's arrival was meant to have finished it.

"Ah, Bascombe. He lives at the end of Gladstone Road. Not sure of the number."

"Good," said Mr Jamieson. "You check with him. We'll have dinner. It's been a long day."

Maddie raised a questioning eyebrow at Esson. Did he want to bring in the scrap of paper? For answer, he simply turned back to the Jamiesons.

"Thank you. I'm sorry, Mrs Jamieson, that we came at such an awkward time. And Alex, if we think of anything more, we'll be in touch. OK?"

Alex, who could think of nothing worse, nodded unhappily. His father gave him an odd look.

Back in the car, Maddie expressed the view that if mother was partially in the dark, father was totally so.

"Agreed," said Esson. "Is it because of what the three got up to or because of what they know about Roger? Alex did not want to talk about him, did he?"

"Both of those things, I would guess. Why did you not bring out the bit of paper, sir?"

"Not sure. Perhaps we had gone far enough. Perhaps we can make better use of it tomorrow, in front of the three youngsters, all together."

Maddie nodded. He drew out his phone.

"Anson. An address please — name of Bascombe, Leura. Probably Gladstone." He listened, then simply said to Provis, "162B." They drove off.

"It is a question," she said, "of whether they ring Bertie before we can get there."

He nodded, then grinned. "And that depends on father Jamieson. Does he insist on them all sitting down to the famous curry? He doesn't know much yet and his ignorance might help us."

Within five minutes they were knocking on another door. It was opened by an elderly man in trousers and a rather worn cardigan. He peered out at them.

"Yes?" He had his hand on the heavy screen security door but he did not unlock it.

"Mr Bascombe?" There was a nod. Esson explained their visit. "We are talking to anyone who might have been in the vicinity of the tragic accident at the Pool of Siloam yesterday. You've heard about it? We think Bertie might have been around."

The man took in the ID and unsnibbed the door.

"I think you are mistaken," he said. "Bertie went all the way to Parramatta yesterday. Something for his Design and Tech project. He didn't get back until after five. I'll call him."

He did and a brawny youth came out of a room further down the passage. He looked at his… what was the relationship?

"Bertie," said the older man, who was surely in his seventies, "these police officers are looking into the death at Siloam yesterday. I've told them you were down in Parramatta. That's right, isn't it?"

Bertie nodded vigorously. The four of them were still standing in the narrow front foyer and nobody suggested moving.

"My name's Esson, Bertie. It's actually not you we want to know about — rather, it's a car, belonging to a friend of yours, Alex Jamieson. You might know something about that, perhaps."

The boy looked surprised.

"Well, yes and no. The car was here while Alex and the girls were on their camp-out for study. A dumb idea, if you ask me."

Maddie assumed he was referring to the whole camp-out idea, not merely to the location of the car.

"Go on. Why was the car left here?" Esson tried to contain his excitement.

"Well, you wouldn't leave it out overnight at Gordon Falls. Here was safer. We are just off the entry," and he gestured vaguely, "to the eastern end of the track."

"The car was here, and you took it to them. When was that?"

Now Bertie really was confused.

"No. As I've said, I went to Parramatta. They would have walked out some time and got the car. They didn't bother you about it, did they, Grandpa?"

"I never saw them." Despite his age, the man was brisk and efficient.

"Bertie," said Provis, "when did you get back home?"

"About five-thirty, I think." His grandfather nodded.

"And the car was gone by then?"

"Yes. Is there a problem with all this? It's just what we had arranged. Is the car OK?"

"No, there is no great problem," said Esson. "It's just that it helps us establish people's movements. We'll be…"

He was interrupted by a familiar sound. Bertie fished in his pocket.

"Oh, it's Alex. Please excuse me."

"Sorry to have interrupted your evening, Mr Bascombe. We'll be off."

Back in the car again, Provis looked at her superior.

"Well, Alex was lying — but why? What does it mean?"

"Everything — or nothing, if it only means he didn't want to feel involved. But I'm sure it's more than that. Alex and the girls have walked through the pool area, surely. We'll see the three of them tomorrow and confront them openly. We'll aim for eight, before these walking people arrive. I have to say, Maddie, that I hold no great hopes of them."

Nevertheless, he looked almost happy. They were getting somewhere: the only doubtful point was, where.

"*Gut*, I think," he said with satisfaction. He gave her a sly grin. "Not *sehr gut*, not yet."

XVI

Determined to make the most of their day, and hoping that the weather further west would be a little kinder, the college group set off early. Their program involved stops at Mount York and Hartley in the morning, then on to Lithgow, so that they could come back up on Bell's Line of Road (who would call a place Zig-Zag, they wondered) as far as the gardens at Mount Tomah. They rugged up in every layer of clothing they possessed and decided to be cheerful. Not ignorance, but forgetfulness, if only for a short time: that was the kind of bliss they sought.

Dennis Millane was part of the group. For a time, it had seemed that he might remain behind but he was eventually persuaded that he would be better off coming with the others. On waking that morning, he had been doubtful, apprehensive.

"Fred, tell them I'm sure that I'm better off here," had been his first offering.

"Ooh, I don't think so, Mr Millane. You need company, and we'll see lots to take your mind off things. It'll be an empty, miserable day back here.

Anyway, I must see that the boys are up. And you'll be better up too."

He gave a hearty, "Good morning. Breakfast in twenty minutes" to the dormitories and then came across the two male teachers checking over their materials for the day.

"Morning, Fred," said Bill Dawson. "Sleep well? And Dennis, too?"

"I think," said Fred, "that you might look in on him. He's set to mope here for the day, but it won't do him any good."

Dawson took the point — "I'll be right along" — and somehow his breezy optimism had worked where common sense had not.

"I'm not sure how far off the main track we'll get today, Dennis, but imagine if you could head home having seen some Wollemi pines in the wild!"

It was a good thing Guy Somerville was not there to hear such nonsense. Millane also knew it would not be so but Dawson's energy was irresistible. He forced himself into action, made it to the shower and dragged himself to breakfast. There, the bounce and good will of most of the boys gave him just enough hope to get him to the bus; once he was aboard, there was no turning back.

"We are not Mr Masterson's history class," boomed Somerville as they drew near to the village of Mount Victoria, "but I want you to try to imagine what this landscape must have been like for the first white people who came through. We are doing it easy!"

In fact, they did do it easy, with short exploratory walks at each stop and plenty of time to inspect landscapes, rocks, villages, plenty of time for eating and for being as normal as they could. It was only at about four-thirty, as they came across the Darling Causeway, that Felicity Madigan could not prevent her thoughts from turning to a probable visit from Inspector Esson in the evening. It was not hard to keep the central fact of Roger's death at bay, but she had remained very aware of Shu and Arty throughout the day. She half smiled as she reflected that she always put them in that order, Shu leading and Arty happily trailing along. She glanced now at Arty. He had managed the day well. He felt things very deeply but he seemed to know when to stop feeling. Maybe he felt calmer with Roger out of the way. That is brutal of me, to think like that, she said, but it was probably true, all the same.

About Shu she was much less certain. He seemed more burdened by the horrible events of Tuesday, or maybe by his own part in them. In Shu she could see the weighty, the debilitating burden of guilt, of how he had betrayed parents, school, himself. Whereas Arty could push it aside, Shu was haunted by his own folly and its possible repercussions. But was it just his stupidity in agreeing to the naked photo that troubled him? She was convinced that the matter of the photo itself would blow over, would be seen as an idiotic moment quickly forgotten. So was he dwelling on something more, something else that had happened at the pool? Could it be what he had done? Or not done? Or seen, and couldn't work out how to respond? If so, could it in some way involve Millane? That might explain both Shu's evident confusion and Millane's wilder reactions. She could not be sure about any of this, but she did know that Shu would need close watching for the remainder of their trip and possibly for some long time thereafter. His kind of deep feeling was really deep churning, and so he gave himself no peace. Felicity did not feel at peace either, and as they approached Katoomba, her anxiety grew and hardened within her.

"Well done, everyone! You've managed expertly today," said Somerville, and Dawson nodded enthusiastically. "We've planned a quiet night; go through all your stuff, photos and all. Then tomorrow we put the assignments together." He paused. "You'll love it!"

Felicity hoped they would. She was afraid that for her, without an assignment to complete, both the night and the long day to follow would only bring on brooding. Then she found Matron South looking kindly at her.

"I think we'll be making our own plans for tomorrow, then, Mrs Madigan."

Felicity smiled back and fervently hoped it would be so simple.

XVII

The young man woke in his Sydney airport hotel room to a grey morning. In such a room, he guessed, it was nearly always grey, because it looked only into a narrow courtyard that was used for deliveries and rubbish skips. What could you expect if you asked for the cheapest room available?

He had booked it for another night, then his flight was on Friday morning. Now he showered and dressed and began to make plans for spending the day. His original plans no longer applied and he trembled suddenly as he remembered why that was so. He took control of himself and turned his thoughts to exploring Sydney. There must be plenty to do in a city of such a great size. He made up a day pack, picked up some tourist leaflets from the foyer and went in search of breakfast. There was a bus stop nearby and next to it a small bakery. It was eight-thirty — coffee and a roll would do for now.

The bus took him to Central Station and he went into the huge hall to look at his leaflets and get his bearings. He discovered that it would be quite a walk up to the area they called The Rocks but it looked interesting and he had all day. Then there was a brochure all about the ferry system. Now, if that wasn't too expensive, it would be an adventurous way to explore. He checked the brochure and decided he could manage a day pass.

He began to walk the length of George Street and as he walked, he looked back over the events of the last few days. He had come with an idea, urgent, imperative, but he had had no plan, not even a vague one, of how to achieve his goal. He knew he had to force a confrontation, but then he had avoided such opportunities as had arisen, even one as obvious as finding his enemy alone in the main street of Katoomba. Perhaps he had known that Roger would not listen, would merely smile that horrible, complacent grin of easy superiority. "Why would you come all this way to see me," Roger would have said, "when we can conduct our business so easily in other ways. Perhaps I should be flattered that you were so keen to see me."

Yet he had come all this way to Australia in pursuit, determined to finish the matter. His problem was that he could not envisage what finishing it might mean. And he could not face the thought of failure.

To accomplish his insane design, he had deceived his parents. That had been easy enough: they were quite happy about his taking a week's summer holiday up north. Then, he had found, even before leaving England, that Roger was to join this geological expedition. Roger always communicated — that was how he kept the pressure on. He had ready cash, not a lot, but enough, and a passport last used on a school trip to Switzerland. So he had decided to track Roger, confiding his plans only to his closest friend, David Handley. It had been easy: a cheap hire car could readily keep watch on a brightly coloured school bus. He had allowed himself just a few days, before anyone back home could become suspicious. He had stayed on Roger's track, without, he was sure, being seen, and he convinced himself that he was ready to confront. But he wasn't. He knew where Roger was every step of the way. Often, of course, that stupid college group formed a kind of unwitting protective shield around Roger. Then there were those two Roger seemed to favour: poor kids, he would get them into his clutches soon enough. It even seemed possible that the intense, darker one might do his job for him. Of the tubby one he had no hope. Then he would stop in horror at what he was thinking. Surely he had not come with that in mind? At times these days he hardly knew himself. But he knew enough to be sure that, deep down, he could not go through with it. So why, then, had he come?

He was planning how to track them through Wednesday when he heard the morning news. It was a pitiful motel but its television worked and he had tuned in to one of those desperate morning shows that mix news of entertainers' private lives with doubtful cures for everything from obesity to hiccoughs. But there *was* news: a tragedy in the Blue Mountains, at a pool called

Siloam, a young English visitor had fallen, was dead. The Victorian school group he was with was devastated; the area was sealed off for police investigation. He could barely contain his excitement. His head whirled and for an hour or more he just wanted to hear that same news bulletin over and over again. He tried different channels, afraid that he had misheard initially, but the glorious news was always the same. Whatever had happened — could it have been the dark-haired boy? — his work was done for him. It says something of his state of mind that it never occurred to him that there had been a simple accident. Surely, he was not be the only person alive who wanted Roger out of the way. And now he was free!

So what on earth to do then? He checked out, went into Wentworth Falls, found a wonderful German bakery and sat in the tiny memorial garden by the railway station to eat and to think. It was peaceful there and still too chilly for any holidaymakers to be out, so he had the place to himself. Its very normality calmed him and enabled him to consider his position. Obviously, he was best right out of the area. Two nights in Sydney? He considered his finances and reckoned it was possible. So he had driven down from the mountains, stopping for lunch and a walk in Parramatta, and then found his way to the airport. He returned the hire car, a day early (but what did that matter?) and found his hotel room. For the rest of Wednesday, he had just sat in a state of bewilderment and relief, until hunger had forced him out. From a nearby Thai restaurant he had taken away a large tub of beef and noodles. He tried watching television, but the news was dreary and a re-run of *Inspector Morse in Australia* was not calculated to cheer him. So he had continued to sit. If he had known about prayer, he might have given thanks for his lucky deliverance. As it was, he just sat.

Now here he was, with a day ahead, the weather just starting to clear, his mission accomplished, even if not by him and he felt ready to play the anonymous tourist. Then his flight tomorrow, home on Saturday and nobody the wiser. Roger was dead. That was really all that mattered.

XVIII

Esson had insisted that the interview take place at eight in the morning. It would be awkward but he felt that he had to move quickly. Things had happened that he couldn't yet get a handle on, and that was not tolerable. His optimism of the previous evening was waning and that was not tolerable either. Various German obscenities occurred to him in rapid succession.

They were ushered into the large meeting room at the police station — Alex and his parents, the father looking particularly alert for any impropriety; Fiona and mother; Ginny alone, which was odd, to say the least. Fiona's mother, Mrs Marsh, seemed to be in charge of both the girls. With himself and Maddie Provis, they all settled round a large rectangular table. He had to be forceful.

"You all need to understand that we are hoping simply to get information, to build up our picture of who was where and when. We would eventually have come to see you girls, but we have hastened because, as you will know, Alex has given us some information but he has misled us, has lied to us, and that raises all sorts of questions in our minds. So let's have no more of that.

Let's work out a clear and truthful account of all you know and saw concerning the school group from Victoria. Understood?"

It was, but as soon as Maddie said, "Let's begin at Lyrebird," Mrs Jamieson butted in.

"I only told you what had been planned. Then Carl came in. Nobody lied to you, nobody."

"We were misled — and Alex," and Esson looked straight at the boy, "knew it and did not correct it. I am afraid that there can be no doubt about your intention to mislead, Alex." Mr Jamieson made as though to speak but decided against it. Mrs Jamieson subsided in a flutter. "So let's not play with supposed shades of meaning any more. Let's get on with it. Sergeant?"

Fiona gave a heavy sigh and looked at her mother. Provis took that as a convenient opening.

"So, Fiona, you start us off. Tell us what you observed at Lyrebird when the college party arrived. Give us the full picture."

The girl looked again at her mother, who gave a barely perceptible nod. If you had asked Esson later in the morning, he would have said it had been a sign, a clear sign to tell it all. Fiona did, including an account of how the tubby boy had come across to chat to them. He had been OK but the English one with the camera had been intrusive and arrogant.

"You didn't much like him, then — any of you."

Fiona was not that silly.

"On a two-minute acquaintance? How could we say? All I am saying is that he… well, he didn't come across too well."

Since almost everyone he had spoken too seemed to agree with that view of Roger, Esson decided to leave it there. He would come back to Fiona. She obviously had more to tell.

"They all went on to the pool. What did you all do? Ginny?"

The girl without any parental support was more highly strung, not apparently anxious, but blunt, not wanting to be there.

"We went on with what we were doing before we were interrupted."

"But," said Esson, "not for all that long, I'm thinking."

"We finished the last topic. It only took about twenty minutes. Maybe we were running out of steam, but we all felt it would have been a pity to stop short."

Provis came in there. "And you packed up and left. The weather, Alex, when you left?"

He was at ease with that question. "Coming over cloudy. Still dry."

"Indeed — the rain was a bit later. But now we come to the critical moment." Esson allowed a good pause. "You didn't go back to Gordon Falls reserve. Instead, you went via the pool and on to the Gladstone Road exit, to collect your car. Now, we know that at no time after the college group got there was there no one at the pool. Therefore, you saw something — one person at least, possibly more."

Silence. Esson was prepared to wait. Provis couldn't. "What did you see?"

Fiona had half a word out but Alex came over the top.

"I'm the one who's got us into this mess. Let me tell it." He was agitated, that was clear, but he was still choosing his words carefully, perhaps still considering what he could afford not to say.

He told of how they had reached the viewpoint above the pool and realised that, if they went straight on, they would have to interact with the college kids again. So they stayed put, hoping it would not be for long.

"We had no wish to be involved at all," put in Ginny.

"That's true," Alex went on. "We really didn't. We waited and saw the teacher depart with the sick boy, telling the others to hurry up. Then we saw the two strip and the English one jump up onto the boulder to photograph them. The fatter one dressed quickly and came across, then the darker one, and we assumed they would finally go. But the one on the rock was taunting the others about how he could use the pictures to embarrass them and cause trouble for someone else, too. We heard Parslow and Millane mentioned, but…"

"Sorry to cut in on you, but this is really important. Roger, the English boy who died, is on the rock, the others down below. He has taunted, perhaps threatened them. Exactly what happened next?"

"I think," and Alex went more slowly and deliberately now, trying hard, it seemed, to get it right, "the dark one — his back was to us — said something like, you wouldn't do that, and turned away. Roger was holding the camera strap and swinging it like in triumph and saying that he would. Maybe he was about to jump down from the rock — I don't know. But in swinging the strap, he must have swung too hard and he lost touch with it. It flew into the air, the camera, I mean, and then he really made to leap after it. He slipped and crashed down. He landed awkwardly and then fell back and his head hit the stepping stone. The other two were nearly at the other side of the clearing and they ran back. There, that's what happened."

He seemed very satisfied. Esson didn't bother with a comment, let alone offer praise for evidence clearly given.

"Now Fiona, I'm assuming from up top you saw that Roger was hurt and that the other two went for help. Also, that you didn't go down to the clearing until you saw that they were out of the way. Yes?"

This time the mother placed an arm on her shoulder and nodded again.

"Well, from the way they spoke, all three of them, he didn't seem to be too bad. To be honest, we thought that if he had a busted ankle, it was no more than he deserved." She blushed as she spoke and her mother looked away.

"So the three of you went down. Ginny, what did you see?"

"The boy, in a bit of pain, lying there."

"Come on — and the rest."

"And his backpack, on the sand where he had left it, and the camera where it had fallen when he lost control of it. Stupid jerk."

Provis came in there. "You said you didn't want to be involved. But he saw you — even lying there, he had to have heard you and seen you. Fiona?"

"He called out," she said. "Asked if we had any pain relief for him."

"And...?"

"And Alex said no, we'd drunk it all," sneered Ginny.

The three parents winced.

"And then? You didn't just walk away?"

"No," said Fiona. "I suppose we could have stayed but there was actually nothing we could do. But Alex said that at least we could do a favour to the other boys and he picked up the camera and hurled it down the creek. The fellow Roger held out a hand for it but he couldn't move. And then — please, sir, I really don't know whether I'm ashamed of it or not — we just left him to it."

She was ready to cry — the other two were not. Esson looked at Alex and the boy lowered his eyes.

"Not that it makes much difference now, Alex, but when Roger held out a hand, did he see you throw the camera?"

"What? Well, he wouldn't have seen it because I threw it from on top of the big rock. He could have heard it, but I think he had fainted by then."

"And you left this unconscious lad — surely it doesn't matter whether he 'came over well' or not — alone and made no effort to help in any way. Pick him up? Make him comfortable? Rouse him if he had fainted? See if he still lived?"

"We didn't touch the creep." Ginny's bluntness was shocking. She saw them all staring at her. "No, we didn't touch him. We walked to the car and that was that."

Esson surged on. "Was it really? You didn't lay hands on him, then throw him back down onto the stepping stone? I think you did, Alex, just to teach him a lesson."

The boy looked appalled. Did this man peer into people's secret wishes? His mother gasped. Mr Jamieson said, "Now hold on there. You can't accuse…"

"No!" Alex shouted and jumped to his feet.

"Steady on, Alex," said Esson very firmly. He got up and leaned over towards the lad. "Is that what happened? I reckon it is."

By now Fiona's face was buried in her mother's shoulder and she was sobbing.

"I think you are bullying my son, Inspector."

"I'm after the truth, sir. I didn't get it at your house but I intend to get it here."

"Then you've got it," said Ginny, who spoke without a flicker of movement. "He's told you the truth. He chucked the camera, the boy was out to it, we left."

She seemed instinctively to know how to say little but to say it effectively.

Esson relaxed. A little. Alex got a touch on the arm from his father and sat down.

Maddie said, "And then you went to your car and told nobody, not even when the news broke that the lad had died. You didn't report what you saw in any way. You were uninvolved!" She let it sit there for a moment, then said, "Oh, by the way, you dropped this."

She held out the sheet of paper. Alex went to take it but Ginny spoke first.

"I was carrying a folder of notes and I dropped it. We picked them up — must have missed a sheet."

"It was only just off the path, not very far from the pool. But yes, you missed it. I suppose you went back to the pool, hunting for other sheets."

Ginny just smirked at her. Fiona offered, "No, they all seemed to be where Ginny dropped them, soon after we left the pool on the way to Gladstone. We thought they all dropped in the one spot."

"I see," said Esson. "I can understand your wanting to get away, and fast, so I'm not surprised that something was dropped. Now listen here, you three youngsters, and parents too, I'm calling a halt here. I have many other things to check. But I warn you very solemnly, if further evidence shows you have lied to us — or misled us — again, watch out." Then he turned directly to Alex. "A fine way not to get involved!"

Alex had got over his earlier anger, or outrage, or whatever it had been and was now mired in lost assurance of himself.

"But that is really what we wanted. Truly. What I can't understand," (Ginny was looking at him now with pity, or possibly contempt) "is why I even bothered with the camera. I just felt such…"

He could get no further. "Come on, boy," said his father. "Enough now. Let's get home."

Provis saw them all out and then came back to the meeting room. She saw that Esson was still in his chair.

"I'm inclined to believe them, especially because Fiona seems the one most likely to tell the truth."

"Yes," he sighed. "I suspect we have destroyed some relationships this morning — or they did it to themselves. Fiona won't be having much to do with the other two from now on, which is a pity for them."

"Yes. And Ginny has been infatuated with Alex, but that will be over too."

He nodded. "He's told us the essential truth." But he was fingering the piece of paper, as though something did not quite fit. The moment passed. "And do you know why I believe him? It's because of his last words to us. One moment of macho ugliness just overcame him, just for a second, that was all. And now he can't understand what on earth that means."

Esson would not look at her.

"It's ten to nine, sir."

He sighed again. "Take a car and go meet the train. I'll wait for you here."

She did, and as she stood on the platform, she wondered if all men experienced moments like that that they couldn't explain, outbursts of fury, some weird macho wish to dominate, to give vent to a barely understood antipathy to another of their kind. She was pleased to leave Esson to himself for a few minutes — and that the train was on time.

XIX

The Shillingworths were strong and energetic people. In their early sixties, they were retired (Rose) or able to pick and choose on a very part-time basis (Martin) and they were both fond of the outdoor life. They were members of an orienteering club; they loved to camp in out of the way places; and they had recently founded the Western Sydney Walkers, a rather gentle walking group for people who needed some activity but needed also to be led, or perhaps subtly pushed, into it. Rose organised and Martin pushed and between them, from their house in the mid-west of Sydney, they had collected some ten folk of about their own age. The walks they had arranged over the last few months had not normally been of more than two hours' duration but the group loved them, and why not! All they had to do was turn up with stout shoes, water and a snack and be prepared to enter into lively chat, or to listen to Rose's lively commentary, as they took their slow meandering way over whatever course had been chosen for them. Most of their expeditions had been local, but now they were ready for more adventure. The first Tuesday of the month was their regular date and on Tuesday the fourth they had headed for the Blue Mountains.

Esson had no idea how useful their information might be. It was too much to hope that they might have seen events at the pool and he was by now perfectly satisfied that he knew Tuesday's timeline. He told himself that all information was valuable, and, amazed at how the interview with the teenagers had stirred him, he was determined that this one would be calmness itself. He sat them all down with mugs of tea in a quiet corner of the station's informal meeting room — comfortable chairs, a low table, a feeling of easy friendliness, or as close to it as a police station may be supposed to produce. His first sight of the Shillingworths gave him confidence.

"Over to you, then," he said when they were settled. "I understand you were in the Pool of Siloam area on Tuesday. Fill us in on your afternoon — not only what you saw, but when, if you can be exact about it."

To his surprise, Rose Shillingworth drew out a small notebook, a diary, as it transpired, of their movements.

"On Tuesday," she said, referring to her notes and speaking as though she were giving a formal answer to a parliamentary question on notice, "we were only seven. Perhaps it seemed too far from home for some of our members. But we had not planned anything strenuous — I really think the others could have managed."

There was a slight cough from Martin Shillingworth and she returned to her main subject with a surreptitious glance at her notes. "Our train got into Leura at eleven-thirty. We had some refreshments at a place called Loaves and Fishes…"

Another slight cough. "Dishes. It wasn't a particularly biblical place."

"…which is on the corner of the Mall and the next street down the hill…"

"Megalong Street." He liked everything to be precise. Esson could see the interview taking rather longer than he had planned.

"…and then," Rose continued without missing a beat, "we had a very pleasant stroll through old Leura all the way to the Gordon Falls reserve."

"Arriving there at about…?" said Maddie, who was keeping her own notes. She assumed there would be a definite answer. There was.

"Not about — at exactly 12.47." She was triumphant. "We took a break, examined the view, allowed for a toilet stop because there wouldn't be another one until we got out and some of our members…"

"Perhaps their full medical history is not relevant here," suggested her husband.

She did not like her flow to be interrupted.

"If you say so. We left the reserve at one-forty-five — yes, Inspector, we do give our walkers substantial breaks — and we took the track to Lyrebird Dell. There is a pleasant picnic spot there and we planned to spend a while at it. We bring thermoses as well as water, and various snacks — Martin carries those supplies" — he made a friendly grimace as though his back and shoulders still felt the strain of it — "and then we walked the short distance to Siloam. We…"

"Just a moment, Mrs Shillingworth — pause there," said Esson. "Tell us about the teenagers who were camped at that picnic area. We know three of them were there."

"Ah," came in Mr Shillingworth when Rose seemed reluctant for once. "Indeed, we saw the campsite and a lot of their debris spread around the place. They were keeping the place in a mess. One of our walkers — she is rather of this type, I'm afraid — started to pick up food wrappers and cans and I was just telling her to leave it alone when a very rude voice came from the back of the cave-like area warning us off. I think," and here even Mr Shillingworth seemed reticent, "that the youngsters, we couldn't even tell how many of them, were huddled under sleeping bags and rugs in the cave. Naturally we didn't inspect that area."

"Naturally," confirmed his wife.

"I'm not so sure about that," surmised both Esson and Provis.

"But since they were so unwelcoming, we did not stay long," said Rose.

"So, from your notes, Mrs Shillingworth, when did you leave that picnic area?"

"At exactly 2.20. Yes, we took the next bit slowly, but there is so much to see. Even at our pace, however, we were at the pool by 2.35 and we stayed there to inspect it all for quite some time…"

"And to have the refreshment break we had not felt good about at the Dell," muttered Mr Shillingworth.

Mrs Shillingworth seemed ready to wax lyrical, in tourist guide mode. "It is one of the loveliest spots in the Mountains. The way in which the cliffs loom menacingly over the water's face…"

"We won't disagree with that, Mrs Shillingworth," said Maddie and got an enthusiastic nod from her husband and a mouthed something from Esson which might have been in German. "But what we need to know is, who else did you see?"

"Whom, Sergeant," came sotto voce but virtually automatically.

Mrs Shillingworth was in a less grammatical mood. "Well, there was nobody there. We had the place to ourselves. On a pleasant day — and it didn't rain until much later — one could spend hours looking at the rocks and the plant life. Of course," and she consulted her notebook, "we did not spend hours there…"

"Fortunately," from Martin.

"Why fortunately, sir?" from Maddie.

"We wouldn't have got out in time for the train," as though it were self-evident.

"…not hours there," as though there had been no interruption, "and we were just packing our few things when we heard the noise of a large group. Kids mainly, and very loud voices they had, too. It is terrible how they can spoil a peaceful spot, defile it, one might almost say." She looked around but received no encouragement to pursue the matter of possible defilement. "So we moved off, onto the track that was to lead us out to Gladstone Road. We were barely out of the clearing when Fran — she is one of our best walkers normally — said that she felt a little odd," (from information overload, thought Esson) "and Martin took the main group on while I waited there with her. We could still see the pool area, enough at any rate to see this large group, teachers and students, as I know now, come down and ruin that lovely spot we had so much enjoyed. We do not go in for childish games like skimming stones, you know. Well, in a few moments, Fran was herself again and so we left the area."

Esson reflected that he still loved skimming stones. He could sometimes get to four bounces. But he forced himself to concentrate, even though he was pretty sure that there was nothing new to glean. "And you didn't see the school group again?"

"Not at all." She reflected a moment. "Unless the other fellow was part of it. But that couldn't be — he was coming in the other way."

"What other fellow?" said her husband. "We passed nobody."

"How odd!" said Rose.

Esson was on full alert. Another person in the area at just the crucial time. Quite possibly unconnected with it all — or not. Maybe this longwinded discussion would be fruitful after all.

"Describe this person if you can, please, Mrs Shillingworth."

She had not made notes to guide her and closed her eyes, trusting to memory.

"A young man, about the age of a senior school student, no, probably a little older. He smiled at us as he passed. He must have been heading for the pool. He was dressed in those silly army camouflage things young people like so much. We only saw him for a second, you realise."

Esson did realise, and he could not see any useful follow-up. Instead, he pushed the folder of Roger's photographs towards the Shillingworths. Martin opened it in front of them both. Esson looked forward to their reaction to the naked one.

He said, "Now, just to be sure, look carefully at the photos and confirm for us that this is the school group you saw."

"It certainly is," said Mr Shillingworth. "I recognise the tall teacher. He was the only one I saw properly."

"But when Fran and I stopped, I looked back," put in Rose, "and, yes, I saw him, and a woman teacher, and the boys look right, though I didn't examine them closely." She began to flick through the pile, muttered

"Oh dear!" as she showed one picture to her husband, then said, "No, I don't recognise these three. This is Lyrebird, isn't it?"

"It is," said Maddie, "and those would be the three who were snuggled up at the back of the cave when you came through."

Rose Shillingworth was not listening. "And this, of course, is the other young man, the one I saw in camouflage clothes. Obviously taken at a different time."

"What?" Esson very nearly exploded. "Say that again."

Mrs Shillingworth wanted to tell him to calm down but thought better of it. "Yes, this is undoubtedly the smiling young man Fran and I saw on the path. You didn't meet him, you say, Martin?"

Mr Shillingworth inspected the photo and firmly shook his head.

She continued, "I wonder where he came from, then. He was definitely there. Now let me see, if we left the pool at three-fifteen, and Fran and I stopped for no more than two or three minutes, he must have passed us at about 3.18. More or less," she concluded, annoyed that she could not be more precise.

Esson was itching to get rid of them.

"Nothing else happened? You saw no other groups, or individuals?"

"Nothing." She smiled complacently. "You see, we are a very well organised group. We had ordered two taxis for the end of Gladstone Road at four and I know we were there in good time. We leave nothing to chance."

"And we beat the rain," said Mr Shillingworth, who seemed to have a phobia in that direction.

"You have been extraordinarily helpful," said Esson, who was trying to suppress his excitement. "And now Sergeant Provis will drive you back up to the station, or anywhere else you need to be."

"Our train is not due for another forty minutes. We'll walk into town and get a coffee before the train. I hope you have gained some useful points from us — I do so like to be precise."

"You are the perfect witness." Esson beamed at her. "You notice a lot and you are exact. Thank you so much for your time."

His graceful compliment made Mrs Shillingworth minded to continue the conversation but that was not the plan at all. Esson was just edging them all to the door when Constable Young came in.

"Sir, the full report from the doctor."

He handed it over with great solemnity.

"I'd better turn my attention to this," Esson said with relief. "It's been a pleasure. Sergeant…" And he waved them off in her company.

"Extraordinary people! But there *was* someone else there. Someone Roger knew. And I'll bet the someone knew Roger?"

He sat down to read the report but could not immediately concentrate on it and found himself summing up his morning first. Speed would be essential. The young man recognised by Mrs Shillingworth had to be from Chaddlehangar: he checked the dates for the two photos that Roger had left on his camera from some earlier time. There were just two, and in one of them, this young man was exchanging a package with another person whose back was to the camera. It had all the appearance of another of Roger's compromising photos. And now the person compromised could be placed at the scene of the crime. He was just about jumping off his seat in his impatience.

Maddie seemed to be taking rather a long time. He turned to the report. Like most medical reports, the facts contained in this one told Esson nothing new: fractured ankle, death by blow to the head, internal bleeding, the blow quite clearly the result of colliding with the stepping stone. What about the two gashes to the head? Ah, here: two blows, one fairly minor, one more significant, probably the fatal one. One odd thing, though. The two wounds were not exactly in the same place, but they were very, very close together. What appeared to be the first and more significant one was probably part of the fall from the rock. The second gash? — Richardson could be less sure. The haemorrhaging must have come from the first blow, but the second could well have completed a process already begun. Esson sat back and tried to reconstruct.

The fellow is injured — then somebody, who was being blackmailed by Roger, grabs him, holds him, and then slams him down again in virtually the same position. That would account for it. If so, there were several possibilities that fitted well, at least as to opportunity: Shu and/or Arty straight after the initial fall, Millane when he was with Roger alone, Alex, maybe, if he had still not told the whole truth, or camouflage boy if he waited until the teenagers had left. In each case — well, he was guessing about camouflage boy, and with all of them, if he was honest — there were those vital minutes alone with Roger. He was inclined to dismiss the Shu/Arty possibility. If it was one of them, his instincts were playing him false. But the others? — definitely possible. He needed to discuss his conclusions a little more with the doctor; he needed to see Millane as soon as the college group got in from their day's outing; and he needed to begin tracking down the unknown person. All thought of Roger having had a tragic accident had vanished for him.

"Sorry, sir," said Maddie as she re-entered the room. "I thought the Shillingworths were about to enrol me in their walking group. They've gone — at last."

Ignoring that, he told her of the doctor's report and of his plans for the day. It was only just after ten o'clock. Maddie surprised him on one point.

"Don't take Shu out of consideration, sir. He's a deep boy, that one."

XX

"But it's the middle of the night. We'll follow it up in the morning."

"I know it's the middle of the night where you are, but it is a matter of the greatest urgency. It is possible that this young man, connected to Chaddlehangar school, is still in Australia. If he is, he will be trying to get out and we have to find him first."

There was a patient sigh from the desk sergeant at Tavistock police station. To receive a faxed photo and to take it to the ferocious Mr Arthur Flint, at such an hour? — out of the question. The Australian voice was continuing.

"The Head of the school already knows of the incident, the death of his former pupil Roger Xanthius. He will surely want to help us all he can."

"Let me make a suggestion, sir," came the pedantic response. "I can't leave my post, but I'll see if I can raise one of our senior people. A couple of them know Mr Flint well enough to be able to make the visit. If you send the fax and then call me in, shall we say, an hour, I may possibly have news for you."

Esson had no option but to accept that offer. It would be a long hour! He went to find Maddie Provis.

"We've sent the photo to the airport authorities, Melbourne and Brisbane as well, just in case, and to the airlines and to the major airport hotels. No response yet."

He frowned. "We are so close, I sense it, and yet we can do nothing." He came to a decision. "I'm to ring England again in an hour. Let's visit Dr Richardson and check out our conclusions with him." He saw her questioning glance. "It'll make me feel as though I'm achieving something."

But you can't always see a doctor, not even a police doctor, whenever you wish it. The wait of twenty minutes was almost too much for Esson, and when Richardson finally appeared, Esson was in what may be called a feisty mood, a mood not improved by the doctor's very obvious geniality.

"I've solved it all for you, have I? Now that I think of it, I haven't. What a pity!" Eventually he perceived that his breeziness was out of place. "What can I do for you, Craig?"

"You can cut the crap and tell us if we're on the right track."

Maddie shook her head in despair. It had always been fun to work with Craig Esson, but this was not the man she thought she knew. He was wanting to surge ahead, without full command of the facts. And worse, he had even stopped using German!

"Come in and sit down. If you're lucky, I'll have some cold water to throw over you." Richardson turned his back on them and led the way into his office. When he faced back at the police officers, he was relieved to see Esson looking anxious, perhaps even mortified. But he would not let him off easily.

"I'm really very…"

"Now, this case of yours," and he cut him off. "In one sense the medical evidence is simple — couldn't be more so. Your problem is what to make of it. I suggest to you, Inspector, that from your point of view, it might mean nothing at all."

Just as intended, that put Esson back into sensible, analytical mode.

"You'll need to explain that. From our point of view, as you put it, it looks like…"

"Let me explain, then. You'll forgive me, Sergeant, if I keep it simple enough for even this bundle of nerves to take in."

He waited a beat, or three.

"OK," said Esson. "I'm listening."

"Then consider this. The interesting feature is that there are two wounds. Well, more particularly, that there are two wounds clearly caused by the same piece of rock and which are almost, but not quite, in the same place."

Esson became eager. "And that makes me think…"

"I wish you wouldn't; I know how you think. I was going to come and see you later today anyway. You see it as evidence that some person grabbed the young man and thrust or possibly just dropped him down so that his head struck the rock very hard, a second blow. Perhaps they barely lifted him, which is why the wounds are so close together. And you think that that action brought about the chap's death." Another beat. "But you're forgetting about the ankle."

Now Esson was truly puzzled. "What about the ankle?"

"You see," in a slow and pedantic manner and with a sidelong glance at Provis, "you ought to consider the possibility that an injured person will naturally try to get up. And if he did try, with the ankle as bad as it was, he might barely have moved before he felt excruciating pain, and then he might have collapsed straight back down and struck his head that way. On the very sharp corner of that steppingstone, and on top of the first, the more serious blow, it might have been enough."

Esson was silent. It was Provis who spoke. "You're saying that his death could have been purely accidental. Of the two scenarios you've just given, are you saying you can't tell one way or the other?"

He did not so much as cast a look in Esson's direction.

"I knew I should have dealt with you from the start. Yes, that is the nub of it. And you — both of you — need to know that, if I were asked such a question as that in court, I would have to say that I can't tell — that, on the medical evidence we have, it is impossible to tell."

Esson came out of his brooding state.

"So then, if it is a crime we are looking at, we will have to find evidence other than that. Fine! Then let me ask you something else. The Englishman Millane says that he attempted CPR: is there any way to confirm that, or to rule it out?"

Richardson frowned. "Yes, I was left a note about that. All I can say is that there is no evidence of broken or cracked ribs. I cannot give you a definite answer one way or the other."

Esson sighed and then said to Maddie, "It's just too much of a co-incidence. He's loathed by nearly everyone, he's blackmailing more than one of them, the victims are known to be at the scene, but just by accident he ends up dead." Back to Richardson, he said, "In my experience, that is wildly unlikely. *Unmoglich!*"

("Thank heavens for that!" said Maddie to herself.)

"That," and the doctor was suddenly gentle, "is for you to work out. But you need to know what my examination says — and what it doesn't say."

Esson looked at his watch — nearly eleven.

"Roger's clothing? Did you see it as messed up, attacked maybe?"

"Good try. It was extremely wet; there were no signs of a struggle."

"There wouldn't need to be, if it happened as I suspect. Well, thank you," Esson said. "Your evidence is frustrating but I thank you for it all the same. It's time I tried the English angle again. Come on, Sergeant."

He almost fled, leaving Richardson managing to shake his head at the same time as he shrugged his shoulders. But Esson's unseemly haste meant only this: that if one lead was the merest blind alley, all the more reason to follow up another. He had to be working away at something. And he wasn't to know that there would be more blind alleys.

The desk sergeant at Tavistock was just as ponderous as ever, but he was in a more jovial frame of mind this time.

"Inspector Esson, is it? Well, things have moved on a little here; I hope we can be of some help to you."

There was a pause — an unnecessary one, Esson thought.

"So what have you to tell me? A name? What?"

"DCI Forrest," came back the very patient voice, "was, as it happened, dining with the Flints this very night. When I rang, it seemed he had left them only half an hour or so previously. It was apparently a function for... No, you don't need to know about that, do you?" Esson almost attacked the phone in lieu of his prosaic interlocutor. "Anyway, DCI Forrest dropped in here, collected the faxed photograph and took it to the school."

"And it was a Chaddlehangar student, wasn't it? Probably a past one?"

"Yes, you were certainly on the right track there. And the interesting thing, DCI Forrest reports, is that Mr Flint expressed little surprise. Not so much at the young man's death, please don't misunderstand me, but at his involvement in something unsavoury. It would appear that he had had his doubts about him on a previous occasion, but nothing had been clear, or perhaps not clear enough to warrant investigation. There might have been a fuss, a scandal. That would be awful, too ghastly to contemplate." The man seemed to drift off for a moment, lost in delightful fears. Then he snapped back, "But Mr Flint certainly was not surprised."

He paused again, as though he had covered all the salient points.

"I must have a name," barked Esson, then he tried to be less abrupt. "You'll understand that, useful as the photo is in tracking the person, a name will help us move more quickly. The person may be planning to get out of Australia right now."

The Tavistock man seemed quite unruffled by Esson's sharp tone.

"Of course, sir, I quite understand. The young man's name is Mr Sebastian Quinlan. He will be just nineteen years of age. DCI Forrest wants to know if he should follow up at this end in the morning, seek information from the Quinlan parents, that sort of thing. He asked me to tell you that their profile here is considerable."

Esson had a fleeting vision of this man as an English judge on a particularly gruesome case nevertheless addressing the accused with ineffable courtesy. Were they all so eccentric, so unlike himself? he wondered. Perhaps Tavistock was somewhere in Midsomer county.

"Anything further you can give us will be extremely helpful," he managed. At this point, he did not feel he had to be concerned with considerable social profiles. "For now, that is all."

He rang off before Tavistock could begin another mild and wandering sentence. He did not know that, having replaced the phone, the desk sergeant sighed deeply at this irrefutable evidence of the continuing lack of manners in the colonies.

XXI

When you have both a name and a photograph — and not only that, but a suspect who, perhaps, does not know that he is already being sought — then the search is not hard. Esson and Provis were soon able to establish his hotel for the night and his Singapore Airlines flight in the morning. The only thing they didn't have was Sebastian Quinlan. The airport hotel could only say that he had gone out early — somewhere between eight and nine was all they would commit to — but all his gear was in his room. He had not got wind of his pursuers and hidden himself.

"You'll just go down to the airport hotel and wait for him, won't you?" said Provis.

"No, I can get the airport police to keep watch and hang on to him. He might not turn up for hours. We know he will turn up, so it's not worth hunting for him in the labyrinths of Sydney. And besides, I want to talk to Dennis Millane again, see what he knows of the fellow."

They were taking a break from the office and having one of Lily's best pot pies with salad. They had reviewed what they knew while they were eating.

"Millane, Arty, Shu, Quinlan, Alex: all at the scene one way or another."

"We don't know that yet about Quinlan, sir. We know he was close by and that…"

"Oh, come on, Maddie. The walkers saw him less than fifty metres from the pool area. Where else could he have been going?"

"I'm just saying that we can't be sure. Not yet, anyway."

"It's like with Richardson this morning: we can't be sure of anything. Except perhaps that Roger's dead; nobody seems too worried about that."

"It's a cruel thing to say, sir, but yes, that's the way it is."

"Not so cruel if he was behaving as we think. Even the English Headmaster didn't trust him."

"But that doesn't justify someone killing him, does it?"

Esson took a deep breath. "No, of course it doesn't. But it is human nature to be relieved when a threat is removed, and Roger was a very obvious threat."

They headed back to Katoomba. The first note Esson picked up was to alert him that Anson Shah had some information about Mrs Sheila Xanthius. He hunted Shah down in the informal room, having his lunch. Esson approached him cautiously. Thoughts of the mother and of his conversation with Provis about nobody caring for the son jostled together in his mind.

"Ah, sir," he said, swallowing a hasty mouthful. "Information to us via the Head of Chaddlehangar school that Mrs X is on an Emirates flight that gets in tomorrow, middle of the day. She knows nothing of Australia and wonders how she is to get here."

Esson gave his sergeant a nervous look. "You and I will be in Sydney later today. Could you stay down there and drive the lady up tomorrow? It would be a help."

He got a very weary nod in return.

"Then we'll go down together and I'll get a late train back, or an early one, or maybe I'll still be with you. But I doubt it, if this Quinlan fellow has booked an early flight. He won't want to stay out all night. He will surely be at the hotel later on today."

He turned back to Shah. "Get a message to her through the airline that she will be met off the flight. Poor lady." Then it occurred to him to ask, "What of Mr Xanthius? She's coming alone?"

Shah made a face. "Supposedly in Switzerland; hasn't been tracked down yet. I have the impression that we don't really want him here. Maybe we wouldn't even let him in."

Esson whistled. "Criminal connections?"

"That's what they're saying without saying anything."

"It's an odd family. Well, I have no idea how we can offer any kind of comfort to Mrs Xanthius, but we have to see her. We have to find out if she has any knowledge of her son's little games." He looked at Provis, who was plainly very worried.

"You're not expecting me to interrogate a grieving mother over a ninety-minute car ride, are you? That would not be right."

Her horror at the idea was genuine. She could be a bold interrogator at times, but the person had to know that they were being interrogated. Subjecting a distraught mother to a grilling was not on — and for what purpose? Esson wondered if he could stay down in Sydney instead. After all, the questioning of Sebastian Quinlan was likely to be prolonged, and who could tell when it might start.

"OK, then. Let's see what time it is when we are finished with Quinlan. That interview might solve a lot of our problems."

She gave him the briefest of nods.

"I have to say, Maddie, that I don't want to be away from here for very long. This is still the centre. I think we can be sure of that much."

Another nod from Provis. He decided to put the matter aside for the moment. This empty patch of the day was doing neither of them any good.

At three, with still some time before the college party could be expected back and with no news from the airport police who were watching Quinlan's hotel, there was nevertheless a break in the emptiness. Though it was only six in the morning for him, Mr Flint rang from Chaddlehangar school. Esson's first impression was of a very decided man, used to making things work his way, but perhaps not as ferocious as the Tavistock desk sergeant had led him to believe. But then, mused Esson, social strata might play a greater role over there.

"Inspector Esson — good of you to take my call. I thought it better we should talk in person rather than through intermediaries. I hope we may each be able to fill the other in with regard to this appalling Xanthius business."

It was like being addressed at a convention. The man had made his last phrase, in particular, sound cool to the point of impersonal. What sort of a fellow had this Roger really been?

"Thank you, Mr Flint. I can tell you several things. One is that we simply cannot be sure whether Roger died by accident — there was a fall, we do know that — or by foul play. Another is that later today we expect to be interviewing one Sebastian Quinlan who is in Australia and was not far from the scene of Roger's death on Tuesday. And thirdly, we expect Mrs Xanthius to arrive tomorrow sometime. That will not be easy, will it?"

Esson hoped to draw Flint on both the Xanthius and Quinlan families. For his part, Arthur Flint recognised, or thought he did, a man of method and one who liked clear information — a man of his own sort. He felt he could speak in a similar manner, though always with an eye to Chaddlian confidentiality.

"I can't say I know Mrs Xanthius well. I should say that they are a loose, perhaps even a chaotic, family. Mr Xanthius is more or less absent. Mrs swings between doting on Roger as the epitome of the perfect son and totally ignoring him in favour of social commitments. I can't predict how she will behave with you — anything from indifferent to hysterical."

He paused, feeling that his brief sketch of Mrs Xanthius had given Esson enough to go on. For Esson, however, it was disconcerting without being helpful. He would have to reconsider how he exposed Maddie to such a person.

"And her son Roger, Mr Flint? How would you describe him?"

"Brilliant," came the very confident response, "and unreliable. You never really knew where you stood with Roger. He understood people, but I think he only understood them in order to use them. So he was at once admired for his brilliance, and at the same time, mistrusted."

Once again it came across as a speech to a gathering, this time probably of underlings. It gave a clear enough picture of Roger, but it was surely holding something back.

"Sir, did this using of others come via his photography? Was he a person to resort to blackmail? Or did he just enjoy making others uncomfortable?"

Flint gave what might have been a cough, or a guffaw.

"My word, you've worked him out, haven't you! All of the above. But I have to tell you that we did not have actual evidence of blackmail. Hints from one or two boys, perhaps, but it amounted only to evidence of their dislike or mistrust, that was all."

"In one sense it no longer matters, I suppose." For Esson, events in England might be interesting background, but nothing more. "Of more immediate concern to us is this Quinlan person. What can you tell me there?"

There was a longer pause this time. Esson was just about to follow up.

"An excitable and nervous lad, but under it all utterly decent. I might even say honourable. I cannot imagine Sebastian getting mixed up in anything unsavoury."

Esson took that in. "And yet," he said, "here he is in Australia, apparently following Roger, we must suppose intending a confrontation, or at least a meeting of some sort. We do know that Roger kept a certain photo of Sebastian, and I am assuming that he only did that if he intended to use it in some way." He let that settle. Then, "You've seen the photo. Does it tell you anything?"

"I'm almost sure I can place it, you know. Have you a date for it?"

Esson rummaged in the file.

"Roger has kept this one from all the way back to March, well over a year ago."

"Yes. Well, that puts it in the latter part of his last school year, though not right at the end. The background, when Mr Forrest showed it to me, struck me as very probably in a small wood on the school property. I can say that with confidence because of the shed that I could just see on the left of the photo. So, yes, I think I can say that it was taken at school, in the last year for both boys."

"There was another person in the photo, a person with his back to us. Are you able to tell me anything about that person?" It was a long shot but Mr Flint seemed to be such an accurate witness that it was worth a try.

"Nothing. He (but it could be a she) is not in school uniform, but then neither is Sebastian, so that means nothing." He hesitated. "So you see it could be an older person, or a school-age person. Since it's on the school grounds, I suppose it's another student."

Esson had the photograph in front of him as he listened. Mr Flint's coolness seemed to be a way of distancing the matter from his school. He remembered the desk sergeant's comment about avoiding anything like scandal. He scrutinised it again: the back of someone in a hooded jacket, hood up, and jeans. Hands out to Quinlan. A small parcel — but it was hard to tell who was giver and who receiver. The day was grey. No, there was no way to tell anything more, no way to be sure of anything other than Quinlan.

"Maybe," he said, "my interview with Quinlan later will shed light on that. If he is as honest as you say, he might tell me frankly. It does seem likely that there was something secretive going on."

"You may be right — as you say, it's impossible to tell. But let me say this. Sebastian is an exceptionally decent lad, but under questioning he will become very agitated. You may want to proceed cautiously."

"Well, sir, thank you for that. I shall try to be cautious — in the context of a possible murder inquiry, you understand."

"Of course." Mr Flint decided on a clear change of direction. "I might also fill you in on his family situation. Virtually the reverse of Roger's. Parents together, loving family, two older boys went through the school, Seb treated just a little as the baby of the clan. They are not silly about it, but one can sense it. The parents are doctors — she's a psychiatrist, he a surgeon — and the whole family are high achievers. Did that put pressure on Sebastian? Very probably. Nevertheless, he was always going to do well. As indeed he ultimately did. He has all the makings of a very fine historian. Not medicine, certainly, but then we are all entitled to our own strengths."

And our own weaknesses, too, by the looks of it, thought Esson. He pressed a step further. "Do you happen to know if they know that their boy is in Australia?"

The answer came promptly.

"No idea. Remember that he left school over a year ago and there are no younger siblings. There has been no occasion for contact."

"Left school to do what?"

"A year off, I think." For once, Mr Flint was a little less than definite. "Or work experience, maybe. Something to set him up in his career. But you have Dennis Millane out there with you. He might know. He tutored the boy in English in his last year, if I remember rightly."

That offered Esson a chance to change direction and he took it.

"Mr Millane," he said, more slowly than was his custom, "seems rather to have gone to pieces since the death of Roger. I'm not sure how helpful he will be. I'll ask him, of course. But does that surprise you, his falling apart like this?"

A huge sigh. "Yes, and no. Dennis takes everything so very personally. He is a fine teacher and good with the boys. In my opinion he should keep his distance from them a little more. Not for their sake, you understand, oh no, nothing like that. But he feels their successes and failures too much. It's part of why they have always responded so well to his teaching. He is of the kind that wears its heart a little too much on the sleeve, I should say."

It was a beautifully phrased sentence. Even so, Esson recognised in it some aspects of the Millane he had been dealing with. Flint's portrait of Millane was not, therefore, untrue, but Esson felt that he was being given a very carefully contrived portrait and he began to experience some distrust for this urbane principal. It made him more determined than ever to have another crack at Dennis Millane and get to the root of his involvement in the whole business. He had said to Maddie that the centre of the case was at the pool; he now began to reconsider that view.

"He has gone out with the college group today, which is perhaps a good sign. I shall see him again later this afternoon. As you've said, he might tell me more about Quinlan."

"Dennis is your best lead there. Mr Esson, I need to start my day but I hope all this has been of help to you. Allow me to say, for the sake of everyone, and especially Mrs Xanthius, that we all hope the outcome will be accidental death. But you must do what you must do. Good-bye."

It had been a lengthy conversation, so that its conclusion, designed to push for a particular outcome, felt unnaturally abrupt. Esson supposed that Headmasters, like Police Commissioners, or Prime Ministers, were meant to be always on the job and that Flint had weightier matters of state before him. He sighed and sat back, then realised that Maddie Provis was sitting nearby. He grinned at her.

"Did you hear much of that?"

"Yes — your side of it. It was helpful?"

"I'll tell you over a mug of tea. Then," checking the time, "we go to the motel and wait for them there. I'd like another full round of interviews if there is time, before we go to Sydney."

"Any of the pieces coming together then?"

"*Nein*. Well, maybe a little." He sat back and stretched his legs out comfortably. He was in musing mode. "Remember when I was first down at the pool. It was still early, not dark, but really gloomy. And the water in the pool had no sparkle to it — it was quite black, in fact. When I looked at it, I didn't see a pleasure pool, for paddling or for skimming stones: what I saw was a black surface, with no way of telling what was underneath. Rocks? Snagged branches, all in a tangle? And then I think of Richardson this morning — the evidence is as simple as it could be, on the surface, but we have no idea what it actually means. This whole business is very like the Pool of Siloam, if you ask me. And that applies whether we are thinking of the Australian end of the case, or the English one."

She raised an eyebrow at that: so the conversation with the English principal had stirred some thoughts in Esson after all. "You will enjoy setting all the pieces out in a clear order, sir, when this is all over."

"*Naturlich*," he said. "If indeed we can ever rule a line and say it's all over."

XXII

At just on ten to five, the college bus pulled into the motel carpark. Felicity Madigan was immediately aware of the car with two police officers in it, plainly waiting for her and her group. She had expected them but she still gave a 'not again' sigh. Then she checked back at Dennis, Arty and Shu: yes, all had registered the police presence. One quivered, one blushed and one stiffened. What a pity — they had had such a good day!

Guy Somerville was giving reminders — "collect and organise all your materials, dinner at six thirty" — but Felicity watched Esson and Provis come towards the bus. The Inspector caught her eye and beckoned her out.

"A good day, I trust, Mrs Madigan."

She replied with a curt nod and a raised eyebrow. Surely, she thought, he has learned all he is ever going to learn from them. Or was he still suspicious?

"Mrs Madigan, we've discovered that another member of Roger's school was in Australia, in fact near the pool, on Tuesday and we expect to see him in Sydney this evening. We want to talk to Mr Millane about him first — get the feel of what we will be dealing with."

"And that's all?" Did she speak more with weariness or with anxiety?

"We may ask to talk to the two boys again — depends."

By now most of the college group had left the bus and gone indoors. Millane was last out. "All tidy, Fred," he said. "Thanks for the day." Then he turned towards Felicity with a feeble smile.

He's in reasonable form again, thought Esson.

"A short chat, please, Mr Millane. It's on another matter. Can I explain to you inside? I hope you'll be able to give me background."

"What do you…? On Roger?"

"Not on Roger," said Esson and he directed a very reluctant Millane to the small meeting room. It was not the place he would have chosen — far too many bad vibes for the man opposite him — but it would have to do.

"Call me at any time, Dennis, if you need to," and Felicity headed warily off to her own room.

"I'm at a loss, Inspector." The day of fresh air and exercise had done wonders for the man.

"I can see that. And I'm going to have to fill you in on discoveries of today before I can ask you anything. Now, we know that on Tuesday afternoon, in the Pool of Siloam area at about the time of Roger's accident, there was a young man called Sebastian Quinlan."

Millane started. But all he said was, "Astonishing!"

"We know because some other walkers saw him and identified him from one of Roger's photos. We faxed the photo to your Mr Flint, who has told us a little about Quinlan but has suggested that you knew him quite well. So, before we see Quinlan, what can you tell us about him? What sort of a young man is he? Roger's sort?"

At those last two words, Millane became almost angry.

"Quite the reverse," he snapped. "Sebastian is as nice a student — that's a feeble word for him — as genuine and decent a young man as you could ever work with. Everyone you ask will speak well of him. He may not have been brilliant, not in the way his parents would have liked." The man calmed down as he thought back to his time with Quinlan the student. "Nevertheless, he made some progress with me, but if he had a passion, it was for History. I think his parents must have finally recognised that, because — well, this is how Sebastian put it to me — they engineered a year at GCHQ for him. That would have taken some string pulling."

This is the most purposeful Millane I've dealt with so far, thought Esson.

"I'm going to show you a photograph. It has been taken from Roger's camera and it dates from more than a year ago. Mr Flint thinks it was taken on the school grounds, in a small wood, I think he said." He held out the photo. "It shows us Sebastian Quinlan and somebody else; perhaps they are exchanging a small parcel. It looks like it, doesn't it?"

Millane took the photo. He nodded — yes, that is Quinlan — and handed it back. It seemed to Esson that he had not wanted to look at the other figure in the photo.

"Mr Millane, I understand your concern for this Quinlan lad. But please tell me honestly: to your knowledge, is there any way he could have been involved in something wrong, something illegal, in about March of last year?" He added, "You were one of his teachers then."

"I was more like an extra tutor, really. But illegal, Inspector — what on earth can you be implying?"

"I'm not implying, I'm seeking information. Of course I'll ask Quinlan himself, but it's always good to go in prepared."

"Indeed, it is! But I cannot envisage, not even for a fraction of a second, someone like Sebastian being mixed up in an illegal enterprise. No, Inspector, this picture must be about something else entirely."

Esson sat back for a moment. He positioned the photograph in front of Millane again and gave the smallest of nods to Provis.

"Take another look at the photo, sir," she said. "Please look closely at the other person. Can you tell us anything about that person?"

He examined it carefully enough.

"No. it could be anyone, couldn't it?" He considered again. "I hope I'm not merely guessing, but I don't think it's a student, not an eighteen-year-old."

"Now, that's interesting," came in Esson, "because Mr Flint was perhaps a little evasive on that matter. What has given you that impression?"

"I don't know exactly…" The three heads bent over the photo. "There's something about the stance. It's as if…"

Esson was too eager.

"You don't mean you recognise this person?"

Millane sat back, as though defeated. In truth, however, he was simply not prepared to go any further.

"No. I sense an adult, but I don't really know why."

Esson called a halt soon after that. Millane had recovered from his nervous hysteria, had Esson only known it, as recently as that morning. He was now coherent and in control. He did not seem the kind of man who would break in pieces a second time. Whatever inner turmoil had threatened to rend him apart was now repaired.

When he had gone, Maddie asked, "Do you think he knows? Or at least he has an inkling of who that other person is? It might not matter of course. Chaddlehangar is a long way from here."

Esson nodded. "But surely Quinlan has to tell us. He can't pretend he doesn't know. If he's the honest person they say he is, he'll identify. You may be right in saying it won't affect anything. But you never know

— what if this other person is Roger's target, not Quinlan?"

"That would make it strange for Quinlan to come all this way. Both of them?"

Esson's eyes gleamed. "That would be interesting! Thank you, Sergeant."

She was not sure why she was being thanked. Her look said as much.

"Because you've made me connect what I should have connected before. Flint and Millane, they both have at least some idea of who this person is." He jabbed a finger at the photo. "And if that's the case, then it's a school person. It all fits for Roger. I've no doubt he was capable of targeting two at once."

He smiled happily. It was about a quarter to six. He sat back in his chair, mulling over possibilities, starting to feel confident that he would sleep well that night. Just then, Felicity Madigan entered the room.

"Ah, Mrs Madigan, your Mr Millane looks very much better today."

It was obviously not what she had come in to discuss.

"Yes. He wasn't so good this morning, but the day out has helped." She sat herself down. "I've just been talking to our Headmaster, Allan Parslow. There are some things I can pass on."

"Please do." A beat. "We might have to go suddenly if we get the call I am expecting." He was almost jovial. "Until then," and he spread his arms out in an over-to-you gesture. For one ghastly moment, the gesture reminded her so forcibly of one of Parslow's own that she forgot where she was. It took her a moment to realise why they were both staring at her. Then she smiled.

"Mr Parslow has had an interview with the Brillia parents and a phone conversation with the Fulsoms. From the latter he learned nothing — Arty had never mentioned Roger to them, their boy is not seriously suspected," (Esson tightened suddenly at that) "and so they are just concerned parents. With Shu's parents it's a bit different."

"In what way different? Both boys had opportunity, singly or together, to do harm to Roger. Their motive would be the same."

"Let me explain." She did not want to go there. "Different, in that Mr Brillia reports that Shu had told his parents quite a lot about Roger. He had posted home a photo of himself and Roger, quite a harmless, friendly one, taken by someone else. But then, on a weekend at home, he told father that he found Roger fascinating, fun to be around, but also very disturbing. And — and nobody else here knows of this yet — Shu told his dad that, in a discussion of what sort of a place Chaddlehangar is, Roger, in a too confident moment, said that Mr Millane would be lucky if he ever got back to it. According to Mr Brillia, Shu told him this on a weekend in late May and the comment by Roger had been made shortly before that. It seems to me, though I can't explain it yet, that Dennis, who was supposed to be Roger's minder, was actually one of his targets. He was placed in an appalling position."

She stopped, glad to have such a long statement off her chest. But there was to be no rest.

"Was one of his targets — or, perhaps more likely, became one. An obvious question then is this: to what degree did Millane know he was a target? You can see, of course, why that is so important."

Felicity deflated. Of course she could see. But what she also saw was that, unwittingly, the college had agreed to a plan that placed a decent man in a vulnerable, an impossible position and that this went a long way to explaining his highly emotional state. She said as much.

"But Mrs Madigan, if that is so, why did Millane not experience simple relief, release from agony, at Roger's death? If he had nothing to do with it, why two days later?"

She rose in a burst of anger.

"Because he's a good man. Does your job prevent you from recognising that such people exist?" She sat again. "The unpleasant young man has been put in Dennis's specific charge. He dies, and Dennis's first feelings are of abject failure, as well as horror at an ugly death. He tells himself that he was not where he should have been, virtually that he is culpable. He is the kind of man who takes everything to heart, and so for a while he can get no further than that."

Esson's phone flashed a message. Well done, Shah, he thought. You did not want to interrupt any interview that might be happening, but you had to let me know. He kept half an eye on Madigan as he read, 'Quinlan at Airport Grand. Held in room by Inspector Field. Your movements?'

"Thank you for speaking to us," he said. "We need to go, urgently, down to Sydney. Tonight may clear up many things. For the moment, let me just say that Dennis Millane, is not, in my view, a murderer."

He and Provis got up. They had virtually to go past the police station, so they dropped in, checked details once more with Shah and got him to phone Field with ETA of seven-forty-five, eight if the traffic was bad. Maddie grabbed an emergency bag that she always kept at the station; to her relief, they dropped by Esson's house in Leura and he collected a similar bag. Then they were off on what Esson hoped would be the last leg of a particularly confusing chase.

When they had rushed away, Felicity, with nowhere to rush to and ten minutes before dinner, just sat. She was frightened. Esson had told her that he couldn't see Millane as a murderer. But he had given her no such consolation about Shu or Arty — especially Shu. Should she see them again that night? For once, Felicity Madigan was at a loss.

XXIII

It was close to eight when they pulled into the carpark of the Airport Grand. Esson had to take a ticket to get through the boom gate.

"Remind me to get reception to validate this ticket for us, Maddie. I'm not paying for the privilege at a place like this."

He had said almost nothing to her on the long trip down from the mountains. Lost in his thoughts, weighing up possibilities, he had for once not wanted to organise his ideas aloud. She was content to sit back, her own thoughts occupied not so much by the coming interview, or the one they had just left, as by the notion of Mrs Xanthius. She had had to meet with grieving parents before, but the best part of two hours alone with such a woman in a car would be most uncomfortable. She did not know how she would handle it. Then she remembered that Esson had at least brought his emergency bag with him.

As they locked the car, a uniformed policeman approached them.

"DI Esson? DI Field is expecting you. I'm to take you to a lounge area, then go up and swap with him. He assumes that you and he need to talk before you interview young Quinlan."

A well-rehearsed little speech, thought Esson.

"Sounds very satisfactory. Lead the way."

There was a small sitting area off to the side of reception — the constable's 'lounge' — with, Maddie noticed, a coffee machine. A tall, bearded man was sitting there, but he presently got up, felt in his pocket for keys and moved off to the stairs. They had the area to themselves. She began to fix two mugs of coffee when a huge man, the kind you think of as a front row forward, strode towards them.

"Hello, Craig. I'm Andy Field. We worked once on…"

"I remember it well." He introduced Maddie Provis. This was not the time for reminiscences. "Bring us quickly up to date. Quinlan is here, then? How is he?"

"He's been back here for over two hours now. We approached him, told him we wished to interview him about a serious matter but that we had to keep him here in the hotel until his chief interviewer could arrive. Apart from that, we've told him nothing, so you can imagine the state he's in. Terribly agitated, and I thought about half an hour ago he was about to start on a full confession. But I told him it was better to wait until the man with all the facts arrived. So, no, he's not in a good state. That might be good for you, of course."

"Indeed it might, and I'm not going to beat about the bush. Did you establish how he spent today?"

"Took the ferry to Manly, it seems. Played tourist. He came back here suspecting nothing. And yet he knows why he is being held."

"Of course he does. But thanks for that. If he has had a relaxing day, well, that in itself could tell us something." He glanced at Maddie.

"But he had to fill it in somehow, sir," she said. "What's more, if he is not our murderer, he is entitled to be relaxed."

That was not the view Esson wished to take. He muttered, "Quite. Let's not take anything at face value." He put down his mug. "Terrible coffee, Sergeant. Where's Lily when you need her?"

That comment could do nothing but mystify Field. He led the way up some stairs and through to a dark rear passageway off which the budget rooms opened.

Field raised his eyebrows and commented on the Grand in the hotel's name. "And he booked what is called a small double, which really means a compact single."

Esson nodded, filing away the information. He felt that he already knew quite a lot about Sebastian Quinlan. Field ushered him and Provis into the room and told the constable he could have a break downstairs. A red-faced young man, who had just muted the television, stood before them.

"Mr Quinlan," said Field, as formally as he could, "here are DI Esson and Sergeant Provis from Katoomba. They will lead this interview. OK?"

How could it be anything else but OK? Quinlan wondered and sat back down in the only chair the room afforded. There was no option but for Esson and Provis to sit, gingerly, on the edge of the bed; Field stood leaning against the door. The situation might have looked ridiculous.

In good times, Esson surmised, the fellow in the chair would have presented well: open-faced, neatly groomed, with an easy friendliness. He could see elements of the character described by both Flint and Millane. Just now, however, those qualities were overlaid with a jittery anxiety and with red blotches coming and going. Esson had said he would jump straight in. He did.

"Mr Quinlan, we are here because of a suspicious death in the Blue Mountains two days ago, in the area of the Pool of Siloam, near Leura. We are here because we know you were in the area just when the death occurred. We are here because we know that you knew the dead person, Roger Xanthius, whom you seem to have followed from England. And we know that, with his photographs, he threatened or maybe blackmailed you. So you see, we already know a lot. Therefore, I want your account of your movements on Tuesday from, say, midday onwards."

Quinlan stared at him. "I don't understand…"

"…how we know all that? But we do, so don't deny it and don't waste our time. Take us through Tuesday."

Rather ostentatiously, he opened a notebook as though ready to check off whatever Quinlan might say against the already established facts.

"I can't start on Tuesday, sir. There's more to it than that." The lad was making a supreme effort to remain in control. "But before anything else, I want to tell you that I only heard of Roger's death yesterday morning. Until then I had no idea. You must believe me on that."

"That's asking a lot, under the circumstances." Esson just stared at him. "Well, give us some background, if you must. I doubt you'll tell us anything we don't already know."

Quinlan settled himself just a little. He had gained a point, or maybe just a little breathing space. Esson prepared to interrupt whenever he felt like it.

"Well, all you have just said is quite true. Roger Xanthius," and his expression turned briefly into a frightened grimace, "is... was... one of the nastiest people you could ever meet. He was in my year group at school but I kept well out of his way. You obviously know of his passion for photography. I think he was very talented, but that's beside the point." Esson was about to insist that he stick to the point but Quinlan gathered himself again. "In my last year, in a moment of desperation, stupidity really, I was persuaded to do something wrong, very wrong, and Roger found out about it. How, I cannot tell you. He said he had the evidence and would use it. He did use it, so yes, he was into blackmail. He waited until we had left school. I went for a year's work experience before uni and all through that time he has harassed me, even from Australia. I've paid him and I've paid him, until it wasn't possible to pay any more. Not on my own resources, you understand. Naturally, I couldn't tell my parents anything about it. I determined to have it out with him and yes, I followed him to Australia. That was a dumb thing to do, but I couldn't think…"

The lad ground to a halt. That, Esson thought, is because he has now come to the difficult bit. But there was something about Quinlan that caused Esson to let him take his own time. He decided not to attempt to crash through after all.

"Do you mean you came all this way without a plan? I find that hard to believe."

Quinlan shook his head.

"What is a plan, exactly? I came here to confront him, to make him see… But in fact, I had no idea what that might involve." He took a deep breath. "You see, I have had opportunities over the last few days, but each time I was afraid…"

Unexpectedly, Maddie completed his thought. "…that he would just laugh in your face? Yes, we know a fair bit about Roger."

He was almost grateful to her. His eyes reddened and he made no move to check the onset of tears. He was looking deep within himself when he said, "Yes, that's true. I had to stop him — and yet I knew I couldn't. I didn't have a clue how to do it. What a mess!"

"Of course, there was a way to stop him — kill him."

Esson's words broke Sebastian's introspection.

"But I knew I couldn't, you see," he said in despair. His horror at the policeman's suggestion seemed genuine. Either that or it was a remarkably good act. Esson and Provis remembered that both Flint and Millane had described this young man as thoroughly honest — honourable had been the word. Nevertheless, when such a person slips and does something 'very wrong', anything is possible.

"I don't say you planned it. Given the way he died, I don't think precise planning was possible. But when the opportunity suddenly presented itself, you may have seized it, almost without thinking. That's what happened on Tuesday, isn't it?"

"No!" he shouted. "I don't know what happened at that bloody pool. I wasn't there." He stopped, alarmed at his own vehemence.

"Really?" Esson said with undisguised scepticism. "But we know that you were there. So let's cut the prevarication and go back to where I started — take us through Tuesday afternoon."

"Yes, OK." He was collecting himself once again. "So, I had followed the group. But every time I might have confronted Roger, there were others about and I couldn't. I nearly did on Monday, in the main street of that biggish town, but again I was a coward and ducked away. I think it was the sight of him staring down the main street with his camera at the ready that alarmed me. You'll say that was feeble of me, and I suppose it…"

"Come on, Mr Quinlan. This is getting us nowhere." Esson knew that he had plenty of time, but he did not want the young man to get distracted.

"Yes, well, on Tuesday the same: I knew where they went in the morning, but they stayed as one big group. I followed the bus in the afternoon and when I saw where they were heading, I went back into Leura and bought a good survey map. Your bush," and he looked at Maddie for some reason, "is full of tracks, which can be confusing and I wanted to know exactly where I was. I followed them in a bit — I can show you on my map — to near the Lyrebird place, but there were too many people. So I went on a long loop — I ran it, virtually — and came back in on a track another way. I…"

Maddie saw a way to check his version of events. "Did you see anyone as you came back in on this other track?"

He thought a moment. "Two old ladies having a rest. I'm pretty sure that was all."

For his part, Esson now saw how Mr Shillingworth's party had missed him. He said, "When you saw those two women, you were very close to the pool. But when one of those women looked back, they didn't see you. They only saw the school group. Where were you?"

"The bush is thick there. I came round a bend, saw the school mob arriving, in fact, some were already there, and I ducked into cover." He almost smiled at himself. "I seem to do that a lot."

It was a point to be checked, thought Esson. He hadn't any strong sense of that path, not even as it approached the pool. All his attention had been on the Lyrebird track and the direct path back up to the Gordon Falls reserve.

"Go on. You watched the college people arrive at the pool."

"Yes, and the teacher talked to them, on and on, and after ten or fifteen minutes I could see that there was no hope of confronting Roger then. I went back the way I had come in, back to my car."

Quinlan was lost in himself again, this time in a strange kind of self-recrimination. He wanted to do something, found that he couldn't and he called himself a coward for not doing it. Was it possible, thought Maddie, that Quinlan drew back from action, because it would only make him as corrupt as the one he so detested? Esson was simply exasperated.

"You mean that's all? You didn't stay to see Roger and two other boys alone at the pool, the last to go? You didn't see what they got up to? Come on, now!"

"What do you mean by that?" Quinlan was asking a question about 'got up to' but Esson took him to be referring to his whole speech, as taking offence that he should not be believed.

"I mean that, after expending so much time, money and effort — a huge effort — to be there on the spot, you just went away? You, one of Roger's most aggrieved victims, went away, and by co-incidence, he dies a few minutes later. No, I can't buy that."

"But it's true, sir," was all the boy would say.

"Maybe we can jog your memory then. The folder, please, Sergeant." Esson leafed through and thrust in front of Quinlan the picture of Shu and Arty by the pool. "You must have seen this. You did, didn't you?"

He was astounded at the response. It was one that seemed to recognise a kindred tragic helplessness, a frightening bond of victimhood between himself and the two college boys.

"Those poor kids. How did Roger do it? Over and over. We all fell for it — well, I didn't — he must have tailed me — I didn't agree to the photo — but all the others did, just like these two." He handed the photo back. "He would have used that against them somehow."

His reply was simple and matter of fact. He had not even bothered to say that he had never seen the incident in the photo but it was obvious from the way he spoke. Esson and Provis looked at each other: another false lead. Maybe Richardson was right after all, in which case it had been a waste of time coming here. Maddie took back the photo, put it in the folder then decided on one last throw of the dice.

"You may be interested, Mr Quinlan, in how we came to know about you. We have Roger's camera, and in it was this photograph."

She handed it to him, and to her surprise, noticed the tears well up again. But he was not merely sad this time — hunted would be closer to the mark.

"Yes, he told me he had this." He began to tremble and his colour drained. "Well, it doesn't matter now."

Esson noticed the paleness and wondered if the story behind this photograph could have relevance. He was gentle.

"Tell us about this photo, Sebastian. What exactly does it show?"

The trembling increased. "I can't," said Quinlan but he was shivering uncontrollably.

"You can, and you must. It's all part of what we are investigating. There is a connection — isn't there, Sebastian?"

He could not work out why the boy would be so very agitated, almost to the verge of hysteria, by a request to explain the photograph. They had, after all, discussed it already: surely it was the reason for Sebastian's trip to Australia. It had to be related to the something very wrong to which Sebastian had referred. He tried again, because Quinlan was silent, except for the chattering of the teeth.

"What is it that so terrifies you, Sebastian? What was Roger taking here? Is it about whatever is in the package?"

The trembling increased. Esson waited barely a beat.

"I see it is. Was it something illegal? Was it drugs, perhaps?"

There was almost a snort of derision but it was the briefest interruption to the terrified shivering.

"Don't be ridiculous." He looked desperate. "But I can't tell you. I swore, so I can't."

Maddie edged towards him from her position on the corner of the bed. "That's all very well, Sebastian, but you must be open. You have been in everything else, so why not on this?"

"I just can't. I promised. We both did."

He stopped abruptly. The chattering ceased and he stiffened.

"And who is we?" said Esson. "Who, young man, is the other figure in this photo? And don't be absurd and say you don't know."

The young man sat perfectly still, as though to do so were to resist. Eventually he spoke, at first with some energy but ultimately in bleak despair.

"I can't say... you don't understand... you can't possibly understand. But if it got out! You've got to let it go. Roger is dead, so it can't matter now. Just let it go."

His voice had sunk low. He had stopped, and he desperately wanted it all to stop. Esson could not allow that.

"We know, Sebastian, of your flight out tomorrow. Let me be clear, you will not be on it unless we get to the bottom of this matter. You are withholding information relevant to a murder inquiry," (Esson knew that he was overstating the matter, but so what!) "and we will hold you until you tell us. Who is this dark figure in the photograph?"

He had all but shouted that final question and its effect was to induce breakdown. Maddie looked at her superior in dismay. Was it going to be another male rant? It would be pointless in this case, she realised that.

"I can't tell you. I can't tell you anything more. Just…" but the boy's sudden spurt of wailing died there and he fell forward out of his chair onto the floor, a weeping heap. Esson and Provis looked at each other, one in amazement and one in 'I told you so' mode, then both of them at Andy Field. He intervened.

"Mr Quinlan, we are going to take a break now and we'll get some tea and coffee. Then we'll have to resume. We can't leave it like that."

He summoned the constable, asking him first to find out if any room service was available. He came with news that there was, in a limited way, if they would be so good as to order at reception. (Good of you to repeat the clerk's exact words, thought Esson.) Then two inspectors and one sergeant went in silence back down to the small sitting area.

"See what's manageable, Maddie, and have it sent up in... fifteen minutes. That'll do us here, I think, Andy."

"Well, what are you thinking, Craig? What's it all about?"

"I assume," Esson responded, "that, even with Roger dead and blackmail avoided, the story of the photo, if it gets out, still has the potential to cause disaster. For Sebastian, obviously, maybe also for the dark figure. Because the two of them seem to have promised never to speak of it." He sighed. "And, from the character sketch we've been given of Sebastian, he is normally an open and honest person, but if he has given a promise, especially if there is a lot at stake, he may well stick to it, no matter what."

Maddie announced that tea, coffee and pizza squares would be sent up shortly.

"Straight from the freezer to the microwave to us," said Field and made a face. "Tell me, what do you know of this young man's family?"

"Extremely high fliers, parents and siblings," said Esson. "Sebastian not quite so much so. It is possible that he has been made all too aware of his limitations."

Maddie saw his point before he saw it himself.

"Brilliant! They are a close family. Sir, why don't we say to Sebastian that we have no option but to ring his parents, tell them he is in Australia, let them know what we know, insist to them that he open up? Just letting them know that something is wrong might be the best way to get at the full truth."

Esson grinned fiendishly at her. "I suppose sometimes we are just about into blackmail, too."

She flinched but said, "Isn't it plain that he can't bear the thought of anyone knowing what happened in that photo? Probably his parents - unless, of course, they are in on it."

Maddie felt that she had to say that last bit. Her heart went out to Sebastian Quinlan and she hoped she was not allowing herself to be led into sentimentality. It was just that, to her, Sebastian seemed clearly the victim.

They went back through the dingy passageways. Before they got to Sebastian's door, Esson said to her, "Let him have a bite to eat, relax a little. Then you hit him with it. It will be just as alarming, but he has had enough of me. It's pretty clear that he responds better to you."

"And have you had enough of him, sir?" She was expecting a quick riposte, but none came. She followed up with, "Yes, I think I know what to say. *Gut, ja*?"

Field grinned, though he had no idea at what.

They went in and had only just dismissed the constable when the singularly unappetising refreshments arrived. Quinlan was trying to pretend that he was his normal self again.

"I can never understand pineapple on a pizza. Feels like main course and dessert at once to me."

Esson smiled in what he hoped was a companionable fashion and went on munching. It was well after nine but the evening was by no means over. Something had to come of this. Field, who seemed to be able to stand indefinitely, went back to the door. Maddie sipped some tea and nibbled the edge of a pizza crust.

"Sebastian," she said mildly, "I'm going to tell you how things stand. I shall be honest with you." Did he believe her, she wondered, and did it matter? "We need to know more about that photograph. You won't tell us, because, you say, of a sworn promise. We can't make you. What's more, we can't hold you here for ever. We have no direct evidence that you committed a crime. And so you will be free to take your flight in the morning."

No, he doesn't really believe me, she thought, but he wants to. He desperately wants to.

"You're a sensible young man. You know we have to do our job, which is to follow up everything to do with Roger. In fact, we are going to do that now. We are going to use this phone," pointing to the bedside table, "and ring your parents in England. And we are going to ask them about your being in Australia, about Roger, about blackmail, about everything."

You could only call it despair. He was trapped. The police officers allowed a long moment to pass. Then Esson, sitting nearer to it, reached for the phone, handed it to Provis and said, "You'll do it more kindly than I will, Sergeant. Not that that will make much difference to our friend here."

Another long silence.

"You win," he said. "I'm beaten. Probably for ever."

In the face of that melodramatic utterance, Maddie was not prepared to show any more patience. She pressed nine and got reception. "Room 1106," she said, but she got no further.

"Stop that!" the boy yelled. "Stop it! I've said I'll tell you."

She said, "Sorry to disturb you," and handed the phone back to Esson. Sebastian looked at it sitting on its cradle and then looked at Maddie Provis.

"It will take a bit of explaining. But when I do, and you realise it has nothing to do with Roger's death, then you'll keep it quiet, please, please."

The urgency in his plea was arresting; Field moved uneasily at the door.

"You know we can't make promises of that kind. Investigations lead where they will lead." She smiled at him. "Let's have your explanation, then. Take your time."

Being a mere nineteen, he made as though to grab another pizza square but thought better of it.

"I'm just an OK student," he said. "I'm good at history, middling at some things, not very good at the maths and science subjects. But I've been taking

Biology, 'to keep my options open,' Mum and Dad say. Whatever that means — I don't want any options that might include Biology. But I've tried. Earlier this year, I was falling hopelessly behind, failed a test and there was a huge exam coming. Mum and Dad had interviewed Mr Lawrence, the Biol teacher, and I think — oh, this is awful! — they more or less said that it was up to him to get me through. They expected it. They demanded it. But I just couldn't do it. The more they insisted that I could, the worse I got. I was just terrified of…"

He paused and they allowed him to. Eventually, Maddie said, "And this Mr Lawrence is the other person in the photo?" She received a nod. Field slipped out of the room.

"One evening, a fortnight before the exam, Mr Lawrence came to me during study time. He said he was preparing some special notes for me, to help in my preparation for the exam. I said nothing would help, but he said these notes would." He gulped. "I think I understood what he was saying, but I tried not to. I just don't do things like that."

"But under the pressure of it all, you did, didn't you. And you and Mr Lawrence met in the woods, away from the main part of the school, and he gave you a package. What was in it?"

"If it wasn't the exam paper, it might as well have been. 'Just focus on these aspects of the course and you'll be OK,' he said to me. I did -, and do you know what? — I was. I passed. I got 67%. Life could go on!"

The edge of hysteria was evident again. Life had not gone on, not in the old way. He tried to get back to his narrative.

"One day, just after the results were declared, Roger came and congratulated me. I've said he and I had nothing to do with each other and that's the truth. I was astonished. Then I got a brief, unsigned note — more congratulations, but this time for receiving a small package from a mysterious figure in the woods. And when Roger next looked at me, I knew he knew it all. And since then, it's been hell!"

Not much more needed to be said. Field came back into the room and nodded. Esson took over. He was most impressed with the way Maddie had handled Quinlan, but his own approach would be different.

"Now, you and Mr Lawrence had promised to divulge nothing, yes? Is there any way anybody else could have known?"

"I don't think so." He had that defeated look again — the confession had drained him completely. "If they did, they've never said anything."

"So how could Roger have known?"

There was a flicker. "How did the bastard ever know anything?" Then a collapse. "I haven't a clue. Did he just follow me on spec?"

"Probably. Or not. Roger always seemed to know exactly what he was doing." Until the fall at the pool,

Esson said to himself. He checked the time — ten past ten. "Now Sebastian, you will want to be at the terminal by what, eight in the morning?" An exhausted nod. "We will call on you at seven-thirty," (a sudden startled look from Quinlan) "not to detain you, but in case anything arises overnight on which we have to question you. You must guarantee that you will be here then, or else we put a guard on you, and that shouldn't be necessary, should it?"

"No, sir. And you'll say nothing to my parents, or anyone?"

"Not at the moment. Tell me one thing — where do they think you are? How can you be so far away and they not know about it?"

"They're busy. The north of Scotland would be another world to them, and emails could come from anywhere."

It was enough. Yet, somehow, Esson wondered if the boy was more in the dark than he realised.

"Until seven-thirty then. Get some sleep."

But when they left him, he was just staring into space, idly fingering cold pizza squares.

"Seven-thirty is early, sir," said Maddie as they trudged down the stairs.

He simply went straight to reception and booked two small doubles for the night. He turned then to say good night to Field.

"No news yet, I suppose?"

"Give it time. My office will be spending the night on hotels, flights, immigration. Just as you did with the young fellow."

"Ring me any time — literally."

A nod. It was time for all of them to get some rest.

XXIV

"Adrian Forrest here. Thank you for taking the call. I know it's early."

It was half past five on Friday morning. Esson had been in a deep sleep, the deeper because it had taken him until after two to settle into any sleep at all. He had come to consciousness abruptly, half knocking his phone to the floor in his eagerness to hear from Field. Then it was only the Englishman.

"That's fine. Good of you to ring." He settled himself up against a pillow. "We've made some progress here — I'll fill you in — but what news from you?" He was what you might call nearly coherent. He grabbed a glass of water.

"I'd be interested to know if you've found the Quinlan boy," came the crisp voice.

Esson was ready now. He gave a brisk summary of the long interview of the evening before, ending up with an assertion, almost a firm conviction, that Sebastian Quinlan was not their murderer. He did not at this point tell Forrest that there might not be a murderer at all. He still could not accept that possibility.

"That leaves us searching for this Mr Lawrence. He could be involved."

"I know nothing of him, so I can't help you there. He is not in our files, but we will begin some checks. See if he's still in the UK." Forrest became just a little tentative. "I've made enquiries, very gently, about Quinlan. There is another family I know, the Handleys, friends of the Quinlans, and my information is that young Quinlan took a week's summer holiday from the job he has in Cheltenham. It's hardly more than work experience, but it's with GCHQ, so there must have been some strings pulled to get him that. The fiction is that he has gone to explore the Highlands. There have been emails about gnats in the northwest and pubs in Inverness. The Australian visit, so I am told, is meant to be a secret from those back home. That is how Sebastian set it up."

"Do you imply that it isn't really a secret? Well, it all fits," said Esson. "I think he is a very decent young man thrown into a complete panic by a terrible mistake and then by this Roger chap. Now, if you can, please tell me what would be the consequences of it getting out that Quinlan, in desperation or in fear of his parents, or whatever, committed a fraud in order to pass a crucial exam? Is it just a case of family disgrace? Other implications?"

"Well," said Forrest, taking his time and losing some of his crisp decisiveness, "it depends on how broadly the news spread. At its worst, it would not only compromise his acceptance into a university, but it would place Chaddlehangar in a very bad light, call into question their status as a reliable institution. I don't imagine they would like that."

"I see." And particularly, he thought, if a staff member connived with the boy in the fraud. So it might not be only Roger's blackmail that lay at the bottom of this case, but perhaps a jealously guarded reputation too. He thought back over his conversation with Flint. The man had come across as decisive and forthright, but he had actually committed himself to very little. "I'm much obliged to you. In Sebastian's eyes, the disgrace is mainly personal but I suspect he has been warned about the bigger implications too. He has certainly got himself enmeshed in something more complex than he is aware of. But it's all unravelling and he has no idea of how to handle it."

"Too true." The voice had recovered its earlier smooth equilibrium. "I'll leave you there, but we will look into Lawrence. Good luck."

Forrest had rung off before Esson could respond. He suddenly needed the bathroom. As he stood there, he planned: tea, a message through to Felicity Madigan, yes, a message, he would not ring her at such an early hour, and then waiting around until seven-thirty. And hoping through it all that Field would ring. Further than that he could not see.

Also up very early was Felicity Madigan, in her case because she had never managed to find her way to sleep at all. She had several times felt herself becoming drowsy, her head heavy, only to jolt into full wakefulness at the thought of the boys in her care. Something remained wrong.

"You poor dear. You haven't had a good night. Let me make us some tea." Matron South was ever alert to what was affecting those around her.

"I'm sorry, Matron. It's still dark — not even six yet."

"My normal time for starting the day." She moved quickly into action. No sooner had she made the tea, however, than there was a knock on the door. Because Matron had thrown on a dressing gown, she answered it. She expected, probably, to see one of the college staff, even though it was so early. She had not expected Arty.

"Matron!" He was very worked up. "Is it possible to speak to Mrs Madigan? It's early but I really…"

Matron looked back over her shoulder, ascertained that Felicity was ready, and said, "Steady on, Arty." Then to Felicity she said, "Here? Or somewhere else?" But her colleague was almost at the door.

"What is it, Arty? Come in and shut the door. Sit over there," and she pointed to a chair beside the bench for receiving suitcases. There was little spare space. For much of the night this boy, though not as prominently as his friend Shu, had figured in her wakefulness; that he should appear so unexpectedly made her anxieties of the night feel prophetic.

"Miss, I couldn't wait any longer. I'm really worried about Shu."

So am I, thought Felicity and she fixed Arty with a firm stare. She liked this boy: he was never going to set the world on fire, not in an academic sense anyway; he was perhaps easily led; and yet, to use a hackneyed phrase, he had a good heart. He enjoyed life and he let his enjoyment spread to others. That was worth a lot. His concern for Shu did not surprise her.

"Has anything happened, Arty?"

"Well, no, but he's as jumpy as anything. He isn't eating, he can't sit still, he doesn't even know when I speak to him."

"But Arty, it's been a terrible time for him. If you'll forgive me for putting it like this, he has been exposed to the whole business of Roger's death even more brutally than you have."

Arty blushed but for once consciousness of it did not upset him.

"He was getting over that. And then, somewhere late yesterday, I don't know exactly when, he changed. Suddenly it's either sitting staring at nothing or jumping wildly about the place. And Miss, I don't like it how he stares at Mr Millane."

They both heard Matron's mug put down with almost a crash.

"Go on, Arty."

The boy now found it very difficult to find the words. There was no blush now — rather, a pale horror at what he felt he had to say.

"I said I was worried about Shu. I am. But Miss, it's because, well, I think so, because he is worried about Mr Millane. He is thinking something about Mr Millane and he doesn't know what to do about it."

Oh help! thought Felicity. This isn't part of the job description of an acting deputy.

"And what have you said to him about this, Arty? Anything?"

"I did try, as we were getting ready for bed, but he jumped up and came and pushed me — Shu did, just shoved me down onto the bed and walked off."

The boy's distress was deep and genuine.

"He's there in the dormitory, I hope. He hasn't gone anywhere?"

"Probably still asleep. He needs it."

Yes, that's what I like about Arty, she thought.

"OK. I'll keep a very close eye. Between Matron and me and the other staff, we'll all keep a close eye. I'm glad you came to see me. You can rest assured that no harm will come to Shu. And Arty, when this is all over, Shu will still be your friend. I have no doubt about that."

Arty gave a small smile, of relief that he had unburdened himself perhaps. He got up.

"I feel…" but he did not finish it. He simply left.

"…better, I hope he was going to say," said Matron.

"He'll manage," said Felicity. "Arty does. But Shu — what on earth does he think he knows about Dennis Millane?"

Matron South, not having anything else to do, made more tea. Felicity accepted it absentmindedly, drank it and had a shower. There was no point heading in to breakfast for another fifteen minutes and so she just sat. She recalled Parslow's words from a previous phone call: 'just make sure you bring them all back'. It seemed to her that she would, but almost worse than leaving one or more behind was the thought that she might be returning with a traumatised, a broken boy, a boy she was meant to have protected. But how could she have prevented any of it? She knew well enough that spending time in 'if only things had been different' mode was ultimately destructive.

She found herself looking at kind, steady Matron when she was aware of a beeping from her phone. She reached for it and brought up the message. She stared at it for a moment, hardly taking it in, then she held out the phone for Matron to see.

"Have a look at this. I wonder what it means."

Matron took the phone and read:

Please ask Millane if the unknown person in the photograph could possibly be Biology teacher Mr Lawrence. Ring and tell me his REACTION. Esson.

Matron knew little about the etiquette of messaging. "He shouldn't get you to do his work for him," was her only response.

"No," agreed Felicity, "but I suppose I will." She wondered what sort of bizarre reaction Esson was warning her to expect.

XXV

Seven-thirty came around at last. Of course, thought Esson, I could have knocked him up earlier — I'm the one in charge here, after all. He told himself that he waited until the appointed time out of respect for Maddie, whom he seemed to be asking to do more than was reasonable. But she had been at his door at 7.25.

"Nothing fresh, sir?" was her terse greeting. His look told her there was not. In truth, he had nothing to say to Quinlan that had not been said the previous evening. They went to his door, seeing, in passing, the same tall, bearded man they had come across down at reception.

"Not many people patronise this wing, do they, sir? I think we can see why."

A grunt. Quinlan opened his door to them and they wandered in, but this time, remained standing.

"Have you thought over all our discussion last night, then? Anything to add?" Esson was not in a mood to waste much time. He had said before that he felt he needed to be in Katoomba, at the heart of the matter, and he still felt that way, the strange involvement of Mr Lawrence and Chaddlehangar school notwithstanding.

What more could he possibly hope to get out of Quinlan? The boy should have been the solution to everything — but he wasn't.

"Nothing to add, Inspector. One question, obviously." The young man was determined now.

"No need to ask it — yes, you may catch your flight." Esson was suddenly sick of the fellow, of his ridiculous school on which he could not quite get a handle. He turned towards the door. Maddie stood where she was.

"Sebastian, I have a question. Since you came to Australia, have you seen anything of this Mr Lawrence? Do you know anything of his whereabouts?"

Esson looked back in surprise but stayed silent.

"No, I have not seen him." The boy sat down on the edge of his bed, in the midst of his belongings. He gave a small smile. "Once, in Katoomba — you know, it's weird you should ask this — once I thought I saw him. A man was standing in front of an antiques shop and I saw him from behind and did a double-take. But then I saw him from in front and it was nothing like him at all." He had obviously been most relieved to find it so.

"Humour me, Sebastian," Maddie went on. "Describe the man you did see."

"Well, I don't see... OK, but once I saw it wasn't Mr Lawrence, I didn't take much notice, really." He paused. "Tall, too tall for Mr Lawrence by inches, and with a huge red beard. I couldn't see much else. Long black overcoat."

Esson was frozen by the door, but he managed, "What was it, then, that made you think of Lawrence in the first place?"

"Something in the way he stood, perhaps. I'm not sure now. It doesn't matter."

It might, thought Esson. He said, "Have you booked a hotel bus or a taxi?"

"Bus. Cheaper."

"And your flight is when?"

"Eleven. If it's on time."

"Have a good flight, lad. And don't be alarmed if you see us at the airport. We have other things to check there. Come on, Sergeant."

They were gone in such a hurry that Quinlan could only give the closed door a puzzled look. He finished his packing. He allowed himself the tiniest smile: back home tomorrow and nobody there any the wiser.

Felicity Madigan did do Esson's work for him over breakfast. She had not been put off by the request in the same way Matron had. Something in the case intrigued her, something to do with Chaddlehangar, something that had its origins far beyond the Pool of Siloam. Had she known of Esson's conviction that the pool was the crux of the case, she would tentatively have disagreed with him. She had nearly finished her own breakfast when Dennis Millane came in. He walked by what had become the staff table and went through to the serving area. Felicity waited patiently.

"Dennis," she said at the first pause in his munching, "I have a message from Inspector Esson. Actually, it's a question that he wants me to ask you. The question doesn't mean much to me but it may to you."

He looked at her and the look said that nothing more should be expected of him. "What does he want now?" he said with a mixture of exasperation and resignation.

"He wants to know, Dennis, if the unknown figure in the photograph," and she immediately registered in him something like alarm, "if that person could possibly be a teacher at your school, Mr Lawrence?"

He had masked whatever the alarm might have been. Or she had imagined it.

"What a strange question!" He turned his attention back to the bacon. "Back home, I'll make sure they learn how to get bacon nice and crisp, like this."

"Yes, but his question, Dennis. What do you think?"

He gave a great sigh.

"I haven't the photo in front of me, have I? The height could be right. The stance could be right. But frankly, it could be anyone."

They all knew the order for the day — assignment work for the students and their teachers, sightseeing or resting for the others — and she now asked Millane if he had any particular wishes.

"Particular, Felicity? To get back home. I'm sorry to say it, but there it is. I desperately want to be with Amanda and then be off. I hope you can understand that."

She certainly could and said so. He had not asked her what she would say to Esson. Perhaps he assumed she would simply report him verbatim. But Felicity knew that what Esson wanted was not in fact information but an unguarded reaction. Surely he would not have asked about Lawrence for no reason. Presumably he knew and wanted to see if Millane also knew. So what should she say? There had been that fleeting look of alarm, if that's truly what it was. She had observed very closely, and that look had flashed across Millane's face before she had mentioned the name of Lawrence. From then on, Millane had been composed enough. She could not understand what it all meant. Just tell him the impressions you received, she said to herself. It's up to him to put the pieces together.

That was precisely what Esson was trying to do. He and Provis had rushed to Reception — she had had to make do with hasty congratulations on an inspired line of questioning — and had found a different clerk from the night before. Impatient as he was, Esson felt that he was beginning all over again.

"We need to find out if a Mr Lawrence was a guest here last night. And if he's still here."

He had pushed his way in front of an elderly couple who were wanting to check out.

"Hey!" said the man. "Our bus will be here in a minute. Wait your turn!"

Maddie turned to him, presenting her ID and asking for just a moment's patience.

"Butting in like that," said the woman testily, but Esson already had the information he wanted. Maddie managed the briefest of smiles at the offended couple.

"He left fifteen minutes ago. Taxi."

"The tall bearded man? But that's a disguise, isn't it?"

"It is." He got to the door but then dashed back to the clerk, committing another ghastly offence in the eyes of the elderly couple.

"No wonder they don't usually get co-operation," said the man; there was something about manners from the woman.

"Give me a token, quickly, for the boom gate," Esson barked at a by now rather harassed clerk and then he and Maddie made a very hasty exit, welcomed on all sides. They hadn't even checked out!

"We don't actually know what he does look like, do we sir?"

"He has to check in. We'll find him."

Just at that moment, there was a call from Andy Field.

"Not too early for you, Craig? You may not have to hurry. There is a Mr James Lawrence on an Emirates flight at midday. Business class and booked through to London. Has only been in Australia a few days. Sounds like your man."

"Thanks, Andy. We're on our way into the airport now. We'll nab him."

He rang off and immediately the phone rang again.

"Ah, Mrs Madigan. We'll have to be brief. I am at the airport to speak to this Mr Lawrence. Any reaction from Millane?"

She told him what she could, equivocal as it was.

"So he had already guessed. And what he thought he saw alarmed him," said Esson. "It's vague — I get that — but it strengthens my feeling that all this ties together at Chaddlehangar."

He had no time for more, certainly not time to reflect that his view of the case seemed to be shifting. They rushed into the terminal building.

She let Shu work on his assignment until the morning tea break and then drew him aside.

"We are going to sit in the carpark, in the sun, for a while. I want to talk to you."

It would definitely not be in that interview room, she thought. It had all the wrong associations. Shu looked wary but followed her out.

"Is the assignment looking manageable?" she asked.

"That's not what you want to talk about." He was blunt but also wary.

"You're right." To herself, she murmured, I need to be blunt too, I think. "Shu, before we head back tomorrow, you and I need to debrief. We need to talk over all that has happened. I am sure that it all still bothers you. We are worried for you."

How would he react to that? Not as she had hoped.

"We? Is that you and Arty? Yes, I behaved badly to him last night. He's been to see you, I suppose."

She had thought he was about to open up, but abruptly, he stopped.

"Yes, he did. As a genuine and concerned friend would. He thinks you're brooding on something."

She sat silent. Then he said, "If I am, that's my business."

"And mine, when it affects how a student in my care is behaving."

Still he would not respond. They sat on their bench at the side of the carpark, Felicity becoming resigned to failure. She risked all.

"I think — this is me thinking aloud, Shu, knowing you as I do — I think that something quite specific is weighing on you. It can't be your Geology. It can't be Arty." She waited for a smile at the absurdity of that thought; there was a tiny one. "It could be home and some difficult discussions to be had there, but you love and trust your parents, as they do you. So what else flows from the death of Roger? Look at me, Shu," and she waited until, reluctantly, he did. "Are you worried about Mr Millane?"

He stiffened with the shock of it. Perhaps he was too stunned to answer.

"Speak to me, Shu. Because I think I can reassure you."

Something of hopefulness swept through his eyes and as suddenly was gone.

"He's the only one. One minute alive — the next dead. He's the only one who…"

What he thought was clear enough. Her heart went out to this shattered boy. A simple excursion — studying his beloved rocks — going along with Roger and doing something stupidly daring — that was the sum total of what Shu had engaged for. What he had got was sitting with Roger's dead body and with the only person, in his view, who could have brought about that death. And he had seen that person behaving irrationally, as though communing with his own internal vision of Banquo's ghost. It had been too much for Shu; lacking full information, he had put the pieces together all wrong.

"We have in Mr Millane, Shu, a very decent man," and she went on to explain the vulnerable, detestable position in which Millane had been placed. "The death of Roger has made him question himself. It can have that effect on all of us — and yes, I include myself in that — but on him most profoundly. I can say this to you because he is about to leave us and you need to know that he leaves us a very good man."

"But then, how…?"

"I don't know. That's the inspector's job. Yours is to get back home, talk it all through with your parents and then finish your time at school — finish it in a blaze of glory."

The phrase was over the top, she knew that. But she had to give him confidence that he could move forward. Better to finish here, she thought.

"I'll let you go back to the assignment, then. You'll do it well, won't you?"

His expression told her that it was still easy enough to talk about Geology.

"I'll manage. It would have looked better with Roger's ph…"

He stopped abruptly. Was there to be no escape from this encounter with death and the turmoil it had engendered? He realised that he was still a long way from feeling relief.

"Allow yourself time to deal with all this, Shu. And value Arty — he's a gem."

"I'll chat with him at lunch." He wandered slowly inside, leaving Felicity overwhelmed still by the way in which the life and death of Roger Xanthius had spread tentacles far and wide. But she had no idea how far, or how wide.

XXVI

"Ah, James. You're heading out this morning, your time?"

"Indeed I am. It was good to see John Walters a few days ago. Even better to be leaving. How is Anna, by the way?"

"She's fine. Has spent a couple of nights with us. Now, the boy? — Can I tell his parents he's in the clear?"

"I think so. The local police have spoken to him, twice now, but it appears that he will get his flight. They will probably speak to me, but that's no problem."

"Really? They've tracked you too, then?"

"I have no expectation that the boy could conceal things for very long — he's not that kind."

"I shall feel more comfortable when you have left Australia. Still, if the whole Xanthius business is over and done with, that will help us all. Is it clear what happened to him?"

"As far as I can make out, beautifully unclear. The police assume a Chaddlehangar connection, but I wouldn't be surprised if it came out as an accident. An outrageous convenience, but life can be like that."

"Quite. So nothing to, er, create public disquiet?"

"I am sure not. I am making a lot of assumptions, you understand. They have not spoken to me yet; perhaps they won't."

"Quite. Safe travel, James. Many thanks, from me and from the Quinlans."

"All expenses paid by them, and time with John Walters: it's been a pleasure, sir."

James Lawrence was now an inch or two shorter, clean shaven, dressed impeccably for business-class travel in a loose checked shirt and jeans. He was now having coffee and a croissant and reflecting that one ate at an airport merely to fill in time, not because of the quality of the food. He had satisfied himself that Sebastian Quinlan was ready to board and now he had a couple of hours of doing very little. The bench at which he sat looked out on an arrival area. A Qantas flight landed, another edged out onto the main runway: it was all business as usual.

"Mr Lawrence, isn't it?" A man in a disturbingly crumpled suit stood before him, holding out some sort of identification. He seemed very agitated. "I'd like you to come with us. I don't want to talk in this scrum."

"But I'm waiting for my flight. It might be called soon." He simply sat, holding the coffee, idly fingering the croissant.

"Your flight, sir, is in more than two hours' time. My name is Esson; as you can see, Sergeant Provis and I need to talk to you, and here is not the place."

The man now stood. His look was one of practised bemusement; he did not seem to be at all on edge.

"Well," and he looked more closely at Esson, "this is all very strange." He pushed aside the dry and tasteless croissant. "I'll bring my coffee, with your permission." He hoisted a small cabin bag and followed Esson. Provis brought up the rear.

In a small room, not unlike, Esson realised, the interview room at a certain motel, he got down to business.

"I realise, Mr Lawrence, that time is short. We are looking at a suspicious death, on Tuesday, in the Blue Mountains west of Sydney. You will probably know of it: you will certainly know the dead person, Roger Xanthius."

"A terrible business, terrible. I had no idea that Australia was such a dangerous place."

The smoothness of his irony irritated Esson profoundly. Stay calm, sir, thought Provis.

"We are talking to you because you are one of several persons who were, or might have been, targets of Roger's threats of blackmail."

"Don't be absurd! The boy was not entirely honest, but really…"

"I say that on the basis of facts, Mr Lawrence, not guesses. You were the teacher who secretly gave to your student Sebastian Quinlan advance warning of the content of a crucial Biology exam paper. Roger took a photo of you handing it to Quinlan. He got money out of Quinlan over several months. He was not a nice young man. But even in Australia, sir, we draw the line at murdering not very nice young men. So you see, sir, we know of your involvement."

Lawrence was imperturbable.

"No, sir! You know nothing of the kind. You know young Xanthius photographed me, but I have to tell you that he never approached me about the photo, much less threatened me. You probably know something of Quinlan, a decent enough boy. You do not know of my involvement in Roger's death because, you see, I was not in any way involved."

"Your presence here at just the right time, your disguise at the hotel — these things suggest otherwise."

"As to the latter, yes, I didn't want Sebastian to know I was here. As to the former, I'll put you in touch with Dr Walters of Sydney University's Biology Department, a former associate of mine, with whom I have spent part of the last few days. Is there a day in which you are particularly interested?"

The man was so calm, so unruffled. Of course he knew the death had happened on Tuesday. He didn't need to ask. It was infuriating. Already, Esson knew that it was just another false trail. He did not like his impulse to commit murder — at that moment, either Lawrence or Richardson would do — seeing it as an essentially unworthy thought for a policeman. He gave Provis the briefest of nods, but he could tell she was ready.

"Tuesday of this week," he said to Lawrence.

The man was ready with his answer.

"Tuesday I spent at the university. All day. It was fascinating. There will be more than Dr Walters who can confirm it."

"Give me more details. What did you do on Tuesday?"

This was merely to fill in time. He barely listened as he waited for Provis to return. She did, in only a very few minutes, and gave Esson a confirmatory nod. Esson remained unsatisfied — with the whole business.

"You say you did not want young Quinlan to see you, to recognise you. Why was that?"

"Silly of me, really. It seemed better."

"But why, sir? No harm in a friendly encounter, surely."

"Away from school, one simply leaves school alone."

It was absurd, of course. One didn't adopt such a careful disguise at a moment's notice. Everything had been meticulously prepared, probably by more than just this wretched Lawrence. And the man had been in Katoomba — but on the wrong day. For the moment, Esson had to accept that whatever Lawrence had been up to, it was not what he and Provis were investigating. He got up.

"You know, Mr Lawrence, I suspect that none of you people at Chaddlehangar brought about Roger's death. But Chaddlehangar still bears the responsibility, doesn't it? A tale of betrayal."

Lawrence was not to be tempted.

"I have no idea what you mean. My flight is getting closer — I'll go and wait somewhere more congenial."

He also got up and reached for his cabin bag.

"Don't forget your coffee."

"It's all yours, sir."

"It's only ninety minutes until Mrs Xanthius's flight arrives, sir."

He wasn't listening.

"Any plans, sir? Are you staying here until then?"

"What?" He came out of it. "Yes, yes, of course I am. I'm sorry, Maddie — I'm just putting the pieces together. As far as we ever will, I think."

His phone rang.

"Anson? We'll be with you early to mid-afternoon. With Mrs Xanthius. We have no information that can pin Roger's death on anyone at Chaddlehangar. But they've all been involved. I'd bet my badge on that."

He listened.

"Yes. Yes, her flight is still showing on time. By three at the latest. You arrange it."

He looked at Provis.

"Fiona Marsh and her mother want to see us again."

She nodded. "And you are already thinking…"

"...that I know what the girl will say? That we've wasted two or three days."

"To prepare us for that, sir, maybe we could...."

"*Ja. Gewiss*! Coffee time."

"...and just maybe we could collect our gear and check out of the hotel rooms? Pay for them, even?"

"You have an evil mind, Sergeant. Would I ever try to leave without doing such a thing as that?"

XXVII

At least on this occasion he could say that there was no wasted time. Flight — passport check — luggage collection and customs — all went without a hitch. They found that they were on the motorway before there had been more than the briefest of greetings. Mrs Xanthius seemed content to sit in the back seat alone with her thoughts. They were passing Penrith when she suddenly spoke.

"What are your regulations, sir, about taking a body home?"

Her voice sounded to Esson as though she had needed to steel herself to that question. He explained that he expected his enquiries to be completed very soon and he would see that she got all the help needed to arrange such a sad matter. She gave a just audible 'Mm' and was silent again.

Anson Shah's arrangements were impeccable. Richardson was waiting for them and it was Provis who took Mrs Xanthius in for the formal identification, Provis who escorted her into Lilianfels, Provis who promised to phone her in the morning to go through any issues she might have.

"Do you know when her return flight is, Sergeant?"

She raised an eyebrow at him, but whether at the information she would give or at his doubting her in needing to ask the question, it was hard to tell.

"Sunday afternoon. Airport at two, flight with Emirates at four-fifteen."

"She's pretty calm, isn't she?"

Provis allowed herself a pause before responding.

"She is. Her only child has died in strange circumstances. I think she's doing extremely well. She's holding it all in — in front of us, at any rate."

"I wonder if she knew her son. Or he her."

"Isn't that something we don't really need to know? Something that won't help us and is better left alone?"

"But I can't leave it alone, Maddie. It all ties in — not so much to the death as to the web of betrayal that lies behind the death."

She couldn't think what to say in response. They were in his car outside Lilianfels.

"The Marshes in a few minutes. They will tell us what we don't want to know."

"But sir, it's a good explanation, and much less messy than others."

"You're right. I want to blame somebody, don't I? And since I can't, I seem to want to blame them all."

It wasn't going to be an idle chat, he knew that, so he eschewed the informal area and led Mrs Marsh and her daughter to the sterile interview room. There was no alternative to himself and Provis on one side of the table and mother and Fiona on the other. He had arranged with Maddie to lead the conversation.

"We are interested that you have asked to see us again. What is it that you want to tell us?"

It was surely only Fiona who could say anything of relevance but it was Mrs Marsh who spoke.

"Fiona has been so uneasy, so anxious. She went through it all again with me last night, and that is why we are here."

Maddie nodded. "And is there something, Fiona, you've remembered, or perhaps see differently now?"

Esson applauded silently. The girl looked at her mother, and reassured, began.

"You see, it's just the moment when we — Alex — threw the camera. We had seen the English kid go quiet — fainted, we thought. Then we looked at Alex, not at him, and watched as he threw the camera." She was barely coherent in her anxiety but the drift of her account was plain enough. "Then we looked back at the boy — he was still quiet."

She was now breathing heavily. Mrs Marsh pressed her daughter's hand.

"Go on, Fiona," she said.

"I was looking at Alex when he threw the camera. I really was. I was just so shocked. But I was also aware of the boy. Maybe he wasn't quite out to it, after all. I just sensed that he was aware of what Alex was about to do, that he tried to move, half raised himself and then fell suddenly back. When I looked at him again properly, he was exactly as he had been. Out to it."

Maddie was very ready to help her out.

"And what's really worrying you is that you now feel that that was the moment he died. And that when the three of you walked away, you left a dead body. And that, if Alex had not had the bright idea of throwing the camera, then Roger might not have died. All that's been hard to live with, hasn't it, Fiona?"

They could all see it: Roger on the ground, just aware enough to register what was happening to his camera, hoping, at first, that it was about to be returned to him, then, grasping with horror Alex's true intention, trying to intervene and slumping back in indescribable pain. They could see him, lying still, against the sharp edge of the stepping stone.

The girl was in tears. Esson assumed that they had heard all there was to hear and made to rise. But Mrs Marsh held up a hand. To her daughter she said, "You know how this will only work if you make a clean breast of all of it. Even if it doesn't matter to the Inspector, not any more. It matters to you, Fiona."

Esson's look said that, whatever it was, it certainly did matter. The mother squeezed her daughter's hand but gave her time. Eventually she spoke.

"We had agreed that there was one thing we wouldn't mention. Ginny said that it kept our story neat, and anyway, who could know."

Maddie made an encouraging gesture, as though to draw the girl out, or perhaps to get her over a huge emotional hurdle.

"It has to do with the papers, the ones from our studying, the ones that fell from one of Ginny's folders. We said that they all dropped in one place and so we were surprised that we could have missed one, the one you found. But in fact, they were a bit spread out. It was — Oh hell, Mum, do I have to say this?"

A brief nod and another squeeze was the reply.

"It was… it was Alex who went back over the path leading back to the pool. Most of the papers were just where we were, but Alex saw one a few paces back and said that he would check a little further back still… and we didn't see him for about two minutes… and then he appeared and said that we must have got the lot and we needed to move on. And we agreed not to tell you this bit, because… because…"

The girl broke down again and her mother put an arm right round her and hugged as firmly as she could. Her glance at Esson and Provis spoke eloquently of her desire to protect her daughter and her determination that such protection should be based on truth.

She bent closer to her daughter and whispered, "You've done well, Fiona. And now it's over."

"Is it, Mrs Marsh?" said Esson. "Now there is the question of whether Alex went back to finish the job."

It was a cruel comment and Mrs Marsh looked aghast. "No, Inspector," she said very firmly. "Fiona is convinced that they left the young man already dead at the pool. That is quite enough for her to be distraught about. What she has told you is so that she can feel that she has nothing left to hide. It doesn't alter what clearly happened."

At that point, Fiona seemed suddenly to come back to life.

"Mum's right. But I remember how I used to think that Alex was so clever and bold and daring… And I still want to think that, but…"

"But at what cost, Fiona, at what cost?"

It was Maddie who had come in and who saw how so many of the girl's certainties had been thrown askew by the awful events of Tuesday.

"But you'll get over it." For some reason she was thinking of Shu. "You have great support, and maybe in time you'll come to think that you were actually pretty brave."

The girl did not look at Maddie — she simply leaned more closely against her mother. Mrs Marsh asked if they could leave it at that for the moment. Esson nodded and seemed to sink back into some inner contemplation. How was he to follow this up? Confront Alex with it? He could not see how he could expose Fiona Marsh as brutally as that!

When Maddie took them out, the mother paused briefly and asked, "Will there be any further follow-up? With the others, I mean."

"That depends on the Inspector, Mrs Marsh."

"Of course." The woman could not stand much more of this horror. "At least," she managed, "I am convinced that Fiona has told me all of it now. What a mess. What a disastrous mess."

"But things can be learnt from it all, perhaps."

"It's good of you to say so. I take it you mean by me — by me most of all." But that was not what Maddie had meant at all.

Her daughter had walked ahead to the car and the miserable parent now joined her. There were not many for whom Maddie could feel any admiration in this sorry business — but certainly for those two. She returned to the interview room, assuming, correctly, that she would find Esson lost in thought there.

"You didn't want to take it any further, sir?"

"There was no need. You handled that very well."

She was pleased. "So then, is there anything more for us to do? I think we know what happened. And if there is a shade of doubt, about Alex, I mean, Richardson's evidence means that we could never be sure, not enough to mount a case."

He sighed. "Yes, indeed that is so. And that leaves us several things to consider."

"You mean how we follow up with the other two teenagers. Is that a must?"

"It has to be. And then there is Mrs Xanthius. How much does she already know of her son's activities? And how much should she know?"

"And how much is it up to us to tell her anyway? Do we make those judgements? She had no part in her son's death. We should leave her alone."

"But, you see, sometimes we do have to make such judgements. Let's go back to the youngsters. Do I follow up with the bold and fascinating Alex, so as to finalise the issue with him and his parents, let them see that we are fully aware of what went on? And then, going further afield, how much of the underlying corruption at Chaddlehangar do we reveal? I think it is up to us, no, it is incumbent on us, to decide those points."

Maddie was silent a moment. She knew what she had to say.

"Sir, you got overheated with Alex once before. Maybe leave him be. Or leave the Jamiesons to me."

"No, Sergeant. The kid misled us, and he was on the spot of a death and chose to ignore it. He has to learn from these things. And I think he can — I confess I have no hope of the girl Ginny."

She certainly won't learn anything from you, Maddie thought. And not from me or from anyone who looks like authority. She moved on.

"And the English school? How do you propose to deal with them?"

"I don't know yet. I'll talk to Forrest. But first there's our own school: we have to let them know that the death of Roger is explained. They can leave tomorrow free of it all."

"Will they be?" she said. "The guy Millane? The boy Shu? I don't think they will get so easily free of it."

Esson merely nodded, rather bleakly, she thought.

"We'll go over there about five," was all he said.

XXVIII

So now, thought Esson, he had all the threads in his hands. No, almost all — he doubted whether he would ever fully understand all that had gone on at the English school. He could not be sure who knew what. It was clear enough that the school would go to extreme lengths to prevent public disclosure and consequent harm to reputation or enrolments. But as far as he knew, they had caused a vulnerable boy to cheat; they had conspired in an academic fraud. There appeared to be no crime, certainly not one that Esson could investigate. Nevertheless, the whole Chaddlehangar part of the case of Roger Xanthius irritated him profoundly.

He was not less irritable when he got off the phone to Forrest in Tavistock. At least the man had been available at seven-thirty in the morning. Esson gave a brisk summary of what he knew, then he went on to things he would very much like to know.

"The man Lawrence, as I say, is smoothness itself. He clearly felt totally protected, invulnerable. I cannot believe that such an attitude comes from acting on his own. Others higher up the chain must have been a party to it — to the initial deception, maybe to Lawrence being in Australia at all. It all feels like a well-managed operation to me."

"A couple of comments, Inspector Esson." Forrest was not as smooth as Lawrence, but he was also not to be pushed into creating a mountain when there was no sign of even the tiniest molehill of a crime. "I understand your frustration, though it appears to come from the discovery, as good as certain, it seems to me, that no one murdered the lad Xanthius after all. Frankly, I would rejoice in such an outcome. As to Chaddlehangar, it is a school with the most impeccable reputation. I have known Arthur Flint for a very long time and he is the last man to connive at underhand behaviour. So, I shall tell him that his Mr Lawrence has, shall we say, gone rather too far in his support of a student. I am quite confident that he will take the necessary steps."

Was that to be all? Esson was not satisfied.

"You could go further than that. You could find out if Mr Flint knew of the whole deal. You could show him what it has all led to."

"But has it, Inspector? Has anything of the exam paper incident actually led to anything? It has not caused the accidental death of a stupid boy who was threatening two silly students with a compromising photograph half a world away. And who would suffer most if any revelations were made? — It would be the boy Quinlan. Is that really what you want to bring about? Expose him to humiliation, blight his prospects?

No, Inspector Esson, I am quite clear in my own mind: the best thing I can do is to have a quiet chat with Mr Flint and let him do his job. You have done yours, most expertly, I sense, and you have shown that there was no crime. Now I'll do mine and Headmaster Flint will do his. I have full confidence that he will do what has to be done."

Esson didn't, but he decided not to say so.

"I feel for that boy. He has been betrayed into a false position. He almost worked himself up to doing something appalling. It could so easily have become a catastrophe for young Sebastian."

"From what you've told me, he could never have made himself act, not when it came to the point. He has a fine and loyal family. We should all just let him get on with his life."

Forrest's tone made it plain that he too had a life to get on with. Esson suddenly lost any wish to force the issue with him. The conversation was almost as impossible as the one he had endured with James Lawrence.

"I wish you well," he said, "in your discussion with Mr Flint."

"Oh, that will be no problem. Good-bye, Inspector."

Esson put down the phone. No, there would be no problem at the Chaddlehangar end. Not now, not ever, for those who had engineered the disaster. But for

Millane? He went to find Provis and they drove to the motel.

"We intend to leave quite early, at seven if we can manage it. Breakfast of a piece of toast, that's all we've ordered."

"You'll be glad to be away from here, Mrs Madigan. I am sorry your trip has been made so unhappy. I am sorry that we have had to contribute to that unhappiness. But at least we can let you go with the assurance that there was no murder, there was no foul play by any of your party."

"It's important we know that, isn't it? Or rather, since I always did know it, it's important to have that clearly and publicly stated. And that causes me to make a request: please, may I bring Shu in and let him hear from you a plain account of what really happened that afternoon?"

He and Provis betrayed no surprise. They nodded and she went to find the boy.

"You thought he was a deep one, Maddie. That I shouldn't leave him out of account."

"As to deep," replied Provis, "I'm sure I was right. That's why she feels Shu needs to hear the truth from us. I note that she made no mention of the other boy, the much more transparent one."

It was indeed only Shu who came back into the room with Felicity Madigan. The two of them sat on one side of the same table in the same room that had witnessed such alarming conversations over the past few days. Esson and Provis had no option but to sit facing them. But this was no interrogation. Esson nodded briefly to his sergeant.

"Well, Shu," she began, "you will be looking forward to getting home. But Mrs Madigan has asked us to give you the plain facts about Roger's death. It will be painful for you to have to think about it again — but it will be much less painful when you know the truth of the matter. And that truth is that he died by accident, by his head hitting the stepping stone. Not once, but twice."

Shu had looked most uneasy when he had entered, even though Madigan had told him that the police brought nothing of bad news. Provis's last comment made him look at her keenly: it was important that he understood exactly what she was saying.

"You see," she went on, "Roger hit his head, as you and Arty saw, when he first jumped and fell. But he seemed to you not too badly hurt by that fall, except for excruciating pain in his ankle. You and Arty left to get help. There must have been internal bleeding already, but you could not have known that. While you were away, the three teenagers from Lyrebird Dell came by, on the way to their car. In fact, they had seen the whole business of the photo," (Shu winced) "and of Roger's threats to you. They saw the fall. They came and spoke to him. The boy Alex, out of a stupid idea that he was in some way getting vengeance for you two, took the camera and flung it down the creek from the top of the big boulder. Roger was aware of what was happening and he tried to raise himself. He couldn't — the pain was too severe — and he fell back, hard, on the stone. That fall, we are now quite sure, hastened his death. When Mr Millane arrived shortly afterwards, Roger Xanthius was dead. Any attempt by Millane at CPR was well meant — but too late."

Felicity had watched colours and expressions change in Shu's face right throughout that speech. She saw him take a deep breath.

"How do you know all this?"

Esson came in then. "Because of the honesty of one of that group of three. One who was too distressed to keep silent. One who felt that perhaps she could have intervened, could have done something to help Roger. but as with you, there was actually nothing to be done."

The boy looked at his teacher, the one who had believed in him throughout.

"I… So Mr Millane?"

"You can put any thought of Mr Millane being at fault right out of your mind," said Esson. "I think you can see that he too has suffered mightily through all this."

"I see that now," said the boy. But then he looked at Provis as though she was the one who might best understand. "Still, if we hadn't agreed to the stupid photo, then none of this would have happened. Arty and I are still to blame somehow."

"No, Shu. Roger was the one to blame for the way he used people. You thought he would never actually carry out his blackmail threat — but he did, in England, and we have spoken to one of his victims. So my advice is, accept that a horrible accident has happened, accept that you did the right thing in going for help, and be prepared to leave it at that."

"As should we all," came in Felicity. "Partly because it's dinner time for us. Thank you both for your considerate behaviour towards us. But as you said earlier, we are keenly looking forward to being back home."

Yes, enough has been said, thought Esson. His approach, he reflected, had not always been all that considerate, so he gave her a small smile, then stood and shook hands with both teacher and student. Shu was surprised, but Madigan took it as it was meant, as the final signing off. She ushered Shu out and off to dinner.

"I trust this is the last time I ever have to be in this room," muttered Esson as he and Provis headed back to their car. It was dark outside, though not wet. To their surprise, on a bench to the side of the carpark, sat Dennis Millane, all by himself, apparently lost in thought.

"Mrs Madigan tells me it's dinner time," said Esson, aiming for joviality. "We feel much the same."

Millane looked up at him and took the pleasantry for what it was worth.

"Of course," he said, standing up. "I'd been helping Guy to load his specialist equipment into the bus, to save time in the morning. But I should go in now."

He turned to walk away but Esson felt a sudden need.

"Mr Millane, you have suffered terribly these last few days. Please believe me when I say we wish you very well. Like the others, you must be keen to get home, home to England with your family."

Millane turned to face him.

"Yes, desperately keen for family. Keen, I think, for England, because I know it. For Chaddlehangar? — not any more. I thought I knew it too, but all that is gone."

Provis moved away to the car. She could sense that something of importance was about to happen between these two men.

"I am sorry to hear it. I had imagined that you were fully part of the place."

Millane shuddered slightly.

"From the moment you showed me that photo, it all fell apart. James Lawrence would never have done what he did without Mr Flint's knowledge. He is, after all, married to Mr Flint's much younger sister." He paused and gazed up at the night sky. "I shall see Mr Flint on my return and tell him how I feel I have been used. But," and he paused again, "I will have much to discuss with Amanda first. And," and here he struck a determined note, "I am not going to ruin Malta for her."

He came back close to Esson and held out a hand.

"Of course you suspected me, I understand that. And if I'd only done what I should have done — insisted they come with me and Bart, at once — then all this would never have happened. So I am to blame, but not," and he was almost fierce now, "not as much as Chaddlehangar is to blame."

"Good luck with it all," was all Esson could manage. They shook hands and he immediately moved over to the car.

"Did you hear all that, Maddie?"

"Yes." She paused. "Perhaps they all think they are to blame, one way or another."

"*Ja*," said Esson. "But 'if only I had acted differently' is a morass from which it's hard to escape. I hope he can. And Shu. And Fiona Marsh. And even her mother." Suddenly he smiled. "I don't suppose we can all be like Arty."

Maddie returned the smile — even the mention of Arty seemed to have a benign effect on people. "Mr Millane sounded determined — at the end."

"I wish him well. He will need to be resolute when he gets back to Chaddlehangar. You heard the bit about Lawrence being married to Flint's sister? So Flint did know; he has used his teacher most disgracefully." He sighed, but then seemed to brush it all away. He gave her a grin. "And I am determined right now! What do you say to a good dinner? I draw the line at Lilianfels, I can't manage that, but where else do you fancy? You deserve it."

"Silks?" she said in amused mockery at his sudden extravagance.

"Done!" he exclaimed. "I need to be shot of all this for an hour or two. We can go on tidying up the bits of debris tomorrow."

I'll take that as generously meant, thought Maddie. But she hoped she wasn't one of his bits of debris.

The packing was done, the bus ready and waiting for the morning, and Felicity sat quietly by herself in the carpark, ready to make one last telephone call. She would be able to tell Parslow that all was well and that they would be home as expected late the next day. She would have liked to tell him that most of the expedition had been completed as planned, that the students' assignments would be thorough and excellent. And in truth, it would be reasonable enough to say exactly that. But somehow it seemed beside the point, swamped, as their time away had been, by the death of Roger Xanthius and the aftermath of that death.

Felicity was in fact still recovering from the visit of Mrs Xanthius less than an hour before. Naturally, all her son's belongings were in his room, neatly packed, awaiting instructions. Mrs Xanthius had to be taken in, had to open up all his bits and pieces, had to finger them with a gaze that was often somewhere else. But then it occurred to Felicity that the woman was being more methodical than that. She even inspected her son's toiletries bag and removed from a side compartment what looked rather like a USB memory stick. Barely a word was spoken, but Mrs Xanthius had given Felicity a card and asked, as though it were the simplest thing in the world, that the various belongings, together with whatever was still at the college, be forwarded to that address. If the pathetically sad and the businesslike can be supposed to mingle in one person, then Mrs Xanthius pulled it off. Felicity got Fred to stow Roger's things in the bus straight away.

She could not put off the phone call any longer.

"Parslow."

"Good evening, Allan. You will be relieved to know that we are all ready to depart, first thing in the morning."

"Excellent. I knew you'd manage it. And is there to be any, er, continuation of the investigation?"

"Nothing at all," she said with relief. "Except perhaps for shipping Roger's effects back to England."

"I'll let Delaney know. He can see to it. And our boys, Felicity?"

That's where his anxiety lies, she thought, approvingly.

"I think we'll be keeping a close eye on Shu for some time. Otherwise, all is OK, I think. You can never be sure what may be buried deep."

"There may well be some strong feeling of relief, perhaps — er, that it's all over, that's what I mean."

You mean rather more than that, thought Felicity. She was shocked, even though she knew Parslow's tendencies well enough. He could see most things only from the point of view of his own convenience. The relief he was thinking of was his own. He would console himself by equating his own feelings with the wellbeing of the school.

"That sounds brutal, Allan. For some people, I admit, there will be something like relief. But I have to tell you this, the person most affected is Dennis. His school has treated him very badly; they put him in a shockingly false position. He and Amanda and the little one fly out on Monday and I don't think he's as keen to get home as he might once have been."

"That's something for him to sort out at the Chaddlehangar end." Millane was no longer his concern.

"Yes, Headmaster. I'm sure you will find time to see him and to thank him for all he has done." She decided that enough was enough. "We will phone when two hours away. I hope to be back by the early evening."

"Have a safe trip." That was about as close to warmth as you got with Parslow. She sat back and reflected on a welter of emotions. Had so much really happened over barely more than three days? Her mind ran over every member of her party and she prayed most earnestly for peace of mind for all of them. As she took herself ever so slowly back inside, she acknowledged to herself that, in all that welter of emotions, there had never been much room for grief.

When she sat at the staff table for the evening meal, she had little energy left for conversation. The boys chatted between mouthfuls; Somerville and Dawson spoke happily of how they would follow up in class when term resumed. Felicity could not be so specifically focused. Her mind drifted away from the case of Roger Xanthius to the nature of the school itself — the college, Chaddlehangar, any complex school. They were indeed complex organisms, she thought, with a tendency to act like independent characters in the story, guiding events rather than being guided by them. She managed a smile at Dennis Millane, feeling as she did so desperately sorry for the way in which he had been manipulated. Then Matron was talking to her.

"I've got a thermos for tomorrow, you know. Bought it up in the town on Wednesday. So we can have a nice cup of tea whenever we want it on our journey."

Was that consolation enough for all they had been through? Felicity smiled hesitantly at Matron South and began her meal.

XXIX

They went to the Jamiesons' house at eight on Saturday morning and were successful in finding all three at home. Alex might perhaps have been still in pyjamas, but with tracksuits, Esson reckoned, you could never really tell. Provis could.

They were taken through to the large rear room again and were offered coffee.

"No, thank you," said Esson, who already had his mind on something much better at Lily's Pad. "This is only a short visit, really to inform you that all our enquiries are concluded and that Roger Xanthius died, by accident, from the effects of hitting his head against one of those huge stepping stones. It is fair that you be told that, and perhaps you would pass it on to the two girls and their families as well."

Mrs Jamieson looked lovingly at her son. Mr Jamieson rubbed his hands together energetically and was about to get up, as though the conversation must already be at an end.

"But *how* do you know?" butted in Alex. "How is it that you are so sure?"

It was a perfectly fair question. But it was not their intention to let him blame Fiona. Alex would talk to her later, of course — if Mrs Marsh would let him.

"It is the only conclusion we can come to," said Provis mildly. "It is what the medical evidence suggests, and suggests very plainly. It is all to do with the two head wounds, one almost on top of the other. We think that at some point — perhaps when he saw you lay hands on his precious camera — Roger tried to raise himself, was defeated by the severe pain in the ankle and fell back heavily on the stone. There would have been internal bleeding already, and that second blow was enough. It's the only explanation that makes sense. And there is no conclusive evidence for any other explanation."

Nothing changed for Mrs Jamieson, but father and son were deadly pale.

"Alex, we should leave it there," but the boy ignored his father.

"You think, then," and there was both bitterness and confusion in his voice and in his face, "that we walked away leaving a dead body there? Is that it?"

"That's the truth of the matter," said Esson. "Your action in picking up the camera..."

The unfinished sentence hung there for a long moment. He continued.

"It was precious to him, wasn't it? Maybe he reached out for it but could do nothing and just fell back on the stone. And maybe you knew, or half knew.

Perhaps you glimpsed the terrible truth when you were hunting for the dropped papers, Ginny's study notes."

The boy had gone very red and tried to hide his astonishment by burying his head in his hands. Esson was nearly finished.

"The truth of this business is something you have tried to hide from, from the very beginning. You haven't told me the truth; what's much more important, you haven't told your parents the truth. It's time to start — now."

The two police officers stood, aware that their presence was now more unwelcome than ever. Mrs Jamison, eyes tightly closed, was determined to shut it all out, but Esson could see Mr Jamieson's face, a face full of pain at the realisation that he did not know his son as well as he thought he had.

He said to the father, "There are things we can all learn out of this most unhappy business. It is best we leave you to it."

Nobody saw them out. Esson marched firmly down the path, but near the front door, Maddie looked back and was, somehow, relieved to see that both parents had their arms around a harrowed Alex. He had escaped — but at a mighty cost to all of them.

At Heathrow, having got his luggage and booked his bus, Sebastian found an internet café and decided to check his emails. There wouldn't be much, but it would fill in time. There was one, however, sent from his father, with a dateline of only an hour or two ago.

Dear Sebastian, (for his father, emails were still letters)
As we understand it, you are back in the country now. I don't think you will be surprised to hear that we have tracked your movements, mostly through the good offices of your former teacher, Mr Lawrence. If you are upset by that news, please understand that we have been very worried about you. But all that has happened is now to be put safely and comfortably in the past. We know you well enough to know that, sensitive as you are, you will be brooding on consequences. You must try not to do that; we just want you to move on. You will want to get back to a normal life, but before you head to Cheltenham, please come here for a day or so. We can't be meeting you at Heathrow but we look forward to holding you close once more. Love from Mum and Dad.

He pushed his coffee aside and then made no effort to stop the tears streaming down his face. Followed! — and by the very man who had led him into this horrid mess! He had been right there, in that place called Katoomba, after all. The man standing near the antique shop — he had nearly seen the truth but had been too trusting. As for his parents, who had no time to meet him, they were ready to give him a solid talking to at their convenience. All that stuff about his being sensitive, about moving on, about no consequences! —

They knew nothing of what he had been through and what he had felt, was still feeling. And though he had not been honest with them, in pretending to be on holiday in the Scottish Highlands, they had likewise deceived him. They had even been in league with Mr Smooth himself, the ghastly Lawrence. He hoped they had had to pay him well — Lawrence would have demanded that!

He had his bus ticket on the table in front of him and picked it up. For the moment, since it did not lead to home, it was his most precious possession. He felt betrayed, by all of them; worse, he felt belittled. His parents had known it all, from the start. But how? — he had only told David. Probably they all saw him as weak, to be led and manoeuvred, not worked with. He reached for a paper napkin to wipe his eyes and face.

A waiter of about his own age was clearing tables.

"Bad news, eh?" the young man said.

"Yes. But no — in the long run, the best of news." He went to the bus bay. He would continue in Cheltenham as planned — it was actually quite fun — but the next move he made would be his choice, his alone. He would make sure of it.

Mrs Xanthius was ready to depart. She had felt quite at home at Lilianfels, her kind of place. But she was eager to get back to the life she knew. Australia was too big. Why, by the time she got from Leura to the airport by special bus, she could have traversed half of England.

She checked her passport, cash, ticket. Then she saw in her bag an envelope, a letter she had wanted by her in case — in case of what, she had no idea. It was a solicitor's letter, from a firm acting under instructions from one Dr Quinlan. She had received it on the very day she had heard of Roger's death. It was no longer of any relevance.

After formal preliminaries, it had advised her that their clients, who did not wish to pursue legal redress, would nevertheless have no choice but to do so if her son's activities, in demanding money in a form amounting to blackmail, did not cease. The letter indicated that sufficient evidence, both from their clients and from her son's former school, would be forthcoming and would constitute the clearest of cases. The letter urged her to cause her son to take careful note of these instructions and warnings.

Had she ever known much about her son? she thought. His father, a pompous man in some ways and at heart a crook, had deserted them, but his departure had left her well off. Roger had been too much like his father and because of that she had often wanted to set him aside, whilst at the same time feeling proud of the very boldness that had once fascinated her in her husband. She had left him to do as he liked, knowing him to be clever, and manipulative. She thought the school might have helped, have done what she was too afraid to attempt, but oddly, it had only made matters worse. Though, to be fair, it had left her with time to get on with her own life.

The solicitor's letter, formal as it was, had been hurtful, and all too briefly, saddening. There was nothing for her to do about it now. Perhaps she could have shown it to the Inspector. But there was no point. He knew something, anyway. Why else would he have asked her about Roger's relationships with other students at the school? No, she would take the only course open to her, and go home, to what wasn't really a home at all. And the letter? — she ripped it into shreds. It would soon be thousands of miles in the past. When there is so little to hold one, it is very easy to imagine that one can safely move on.

But then, somehow, she found herself fingering the USB stick that was still in her coat pocket. Destroy it too? There would be unpleasant images on it, she had no doubt of that. Well, she could delete all those. There might be other images there, pictures that would remind her of the brilliant son she had not properly cherished. Yes, she would delete what needed to go. Then she would have the Roger she wanted to remember.

XXX

They went to Richardson's office first.

"Available, for once, I see, Doctor."

Provis thought that Esson could have made a better opening than that. Richardson took it in his stride.

"Only for you. It's in the fridge, second shelf down."

She wasn't quick enough. "What is, Doctor?"

"He means," with a grin of delight at how the game was being played, "my slice of humble pie."

"And don't choke on it — I'm too busy at the moment," said Richardson as Maddie shook with silent laughter. She stood to one side, ready to let them do it their way. Esson needed to get it over with.

"You were right to say that it might just as easily have happened that way. It was a provoked accident, perhaps, but an accident all the same."

He gave a brief account of how Roger reacted to the seizing of his camera.

"It fits. You're not actually sorry about it, are you?"

"Now why does everyone want to pin that on me?" He looked at Maddie and made a ludicrously helpless gesture, but she only shook her head. "Am I as cold-blooded as all that? I was only following up the evidence. I'm a kind enough cop, surely?"

"It's not in your job description to be kind, Craig. But the case needled at you, that's for sure. Why was it so important that someone be to blame?"

"Because," and he pondered a moment, "because they all were."

"All, sir?" She wasn't going to stand for that.

"Lots of them, anyway. But," and he was suddenly eager to move on, "I need to wash the whole unpleasant business off with a huge Lily's breakfast. Come on, Sergeant."

Richardson held up a hand. He put on a cryptic face. "Don't rush. I won't bring out the pie, I promise. It's just that — for a second and fatal hit to the head to be the result of just falling back like that, without any extra force applied: possible, but unusual. Most unusual. That's all I'm going to say."

Maddie gaped at him. Esson was unfazed.

"Much of our job is to come to grips with the unusual. As is yours, Doctor. Once more, come on, Sergeant."

Outside, Maddie could not hold it in.

"Was he suggesting we should be continuing with the case, sir? After all this?"

"No. Just giving me back what I deserved." He gave her what he hoped was a reassuring look. "It's a game he plays, pretending that nothing is ever truly finished. And in a sense, he's right. *Also*, breakfast, *bitte*."

She let it go: objecting to his mixture of tongues would have been churlish.

Lily's Pad satisfied the taste and the appetite of each of them. At first, they just enjoyed time to let the case slide away. But for Esson, just as he had to think out loud along the way, summing up out loud was a necessity too.

"You were right when you called me in, Maddie. The evidence you had did not come together comfortably. So we investigated, and behold, all sorts of fresh complications arose. For a non-murder, it was a very complex case."

He signalled for more coffee. She prodded him. "Is that all you can say about it — a 'non-murder'?"

He nodded approvingly.

"Far from it. If we didn't have a murder — in our jurisdiction, not even a crime — then we did have an intricate, perhaps even a vicious, web of betrayal. If you ever turn into a Dr Watson, Maddie, that's what this narrative will be about. A Study in Betrayal."

"I can see that. But was it all deliberate? Or did some of them just fall into it?"

"Rebellion lay in his way and he found it! No, don't bother to source the quotation, Maddie. Look, we can see actions, but it is not always easy to see intentions. Still," and he gestured approvingly when his second, or maybe third, mug arrived, "there were betrayals of trust all along the line. Millane by his home school, Sebastian by the school and perhaps by his parents too. Then there is Lawrence — I wouldn't trust him for a second. Or young Alex, or his girl Ginny. Shu feels he betrayed parental trust and he was betrayed in turn by Roger, who was deserted, maybe betrayed, by one or both parents. But in his turn, he was prepared to betray everyone." He sighed. "Most of all that was outside our orbit, but it is what drove the case."

"Perhaps that's what crime is, sir — betrayal of one sort or another."

"It's more than that. Greed? Lust for power? Ungovernable rage? Madness? Yes, there is a betrayal of trust in many crimes, but in this case, it was calculated, maliciously manipulative. And except for Roger, the arch-manipulators go unpunished."

I ought to feel relieved at the end of a case, he said to himself. Instead, I feel frustrated. Is Maddie right? — Above all, do I need to feel that there is someone to blame for all the ills of the world? And anyway, am I not a part of all those ills? His initial, irrational antagonism at Alex rose uncomfortably before him. He needed, he knew, to wash this case off, but he also knew that, as with the sporting club business, that might not be so easy. But Maddie was speaking.

"It was a mess. But you unravelled it. That must be worth something."

"We — together," he insisted. "But, you see, it's only unravelled in our minds. People's tangled lives don't unravel so easily."

"Sebastian's? Shu's? Millane's?" She received a nod at each name. "We just need to give them time. The boys will come good."

"Time, yes, but something more. Do you know the loveliest word, in sound and in sense, the Germans use, Maddie?"

What else could she do but raise an eyebrow at him? He stood and found his credit card. When he had settled up, he stood outside in the laneway.

"I'm still waiting for the answer, sir."

"And I'm waiting for it too: *Ruh*."

Some six weeks later, as he concluded a highly satisfactory meeting as Chair of the Academic Committee of South-West Schools, the Headmaster was handed a note by his secretary.

Dear Mr Flint,

It will come as no surprise to you that I have accepted the position in Exeter. My last day of service here will be the last day of this Christmas term, December 16. I had hoped my time here would have been longer and would have ended more happily. It was not to be.

Yours sincerely,
Dennis Millane.

Flint managed a tight smile. It was best — in fact, it was the only way. The Xanthius case was closed, once and for all.

On Sunday, December 18, the weather was much warmer, the water glistening, the creek just trickling round the stepping stones and meandering down into the valley, the boulder high and dry.

The case had come into the mind of Maddie Provis early that morning, as she set off on a vigorous walk. Yes, she said to herself, I can go that way again now. It will be different at this time of year, and somehow, I'd like to observe it once more.

She came in from the Gordon Falls end and took the steep path straight down, as she had done on that very first occasion. Lyrebird Dell crossed her mind and caused a fleeting expression of distaste. She would not go that way. The path was entirely dry and she made a very slight detour to the viewing point before descending to the pool. Siloam? — there was a flash of memory from her school days of Jesus telling a blind man to go and wash in the pool of Siloam. But it wasn't the pool that healed him, it was the man. And this pool, quiet as it now was, could not heal either. On the contrary, as Esson had said to her, it might look calm but perhaps its surface was deceptive, masking all the entanglements that made life such a problem. She smiled at the recollection of how she and Esson had worked that case. Then she took a last look at the pool: it seemed calm indeed, full of peace, of what Esson liked to call *Ruh*. Maddie continued her walk, wondering as she went whether true peace had returned to the lives of those who had been caught up in the horrible mess that swirled around Roger Xanthius. Shu, the deep one? Sebastian, outmanoeuvred by them all? She hoped they were flourishing.

Enough! She headed off towards Gladstone Road and began to run. All of a sudden, her thoughts were of coffee at Lily's Pad.

AUTHOR'S NOTE

The characters and events in this story are all purely fictional. Some years ago, I undertook just such a teaching exchange, as Dennis Millane is part of; and in my teaching career, I worked with several young men in Roger's position. For those young men, and especially for my exchange partner, I have only the highest regard. Similarly, if Chaddlehangar school does not come out of my story smelling all that sweet, that has nothing to do with the wonderful time I was afforded by all associated with Dean Close School in Gloucestershire. Chaddlehangar and its occupants are designed to make the plot work. I can only hope that they do so in a way that is satisfying.